KARMA DECAY

JUDE FAWLEY

STICKS RIVER

STICKS RIVER

This book is a work of fiction. Names, characters, places, and incidents
either are products of the author's imagination or are used fictitiously.
Any resemblance to actual events or locales or persons,
living or dead, is entirely coincidental.

KARMA DECAY

DESIGNED BY KARL PFEIFFER

Text set in the Garamond family

Produced in the United States of America

ISBN-13: 978-1494843939
ISBN-10: 1494843935

REVISED FIRST EDITION

Anti-Dedication

This book is specifically not for Elizabeth—
if you see her reading it, I would appreciate it if you removed it from her hands,
and replaced it with a book she is allowed to read.
I will leave the choice of what that book is to you

KARMA DECAY

1

THE DOOR OF the grocery store opened automatically in front of Aaron, letting out a breeze of air conditioning. A couple was leaving at the same time, and greeted him with a smile as they passed. He always forgot how warm it got outside recently, even in the winter. The seasons were evening out at an alarming rate, he noticed. It was just three years before that they seemed passably different from each other, snowing in the winter and raining in the summer, but lately it always seemed to be somewhere in between, which would have been enjoyable had it not meant that the world was probably ending. The newspapers agreed.

A man was standing by the grocery carts, bodily preventing anyone from taking them without his consent. He didn't work there. As Aaron tried to discreetly grab a handbasket from their stack beside the long rows of carts, the man stepped forward to intercept him. "Here, let me get a cart for you."

"I don't want a cart," Aaron said. "In fact, I was trying to get one of these baskets over here. So if you would please." He meant to imply that the man should step aside, which he felt to be obvious, but the man was strongly insisting.

"You can't fit as much in a handbasket," he said good-humoredly, and let out a coarse laugh. "You don't want to go hungry now. Or hurt your back."

"I'll take my chances."

"Here, let me get one for you then," the man said, adapting. Still firmly blocking Aaron, he turned around to address the stack of baskets. Instead of just taking the one from the top, like a decent human being, the man inspected several, apparently for quality.

Aaron nearly pushed him aside in a fit of impatience, but, after taking a deep breath, was able to just let it happen. When the man finally handed one over, Aaron smiled with thin lips and moved on.

He only needed a few things, a loaf of bread, some cereal and butter. The cheapest things a person could reasonably live on. All of the people he passed on the way seemed to be well on their way to poverty as well, although it might have only been his own perspective. Their clothes were lightly fraying, and their hygiene was a little lacking, but it was mostly the wariness he sensed behind their smiles that made him see poverty in every face. They were always smiling, every one of them—the couple leaving the store, the man trying to offer him a cart, the man that was currently helping Aaron to reach the cereal he wanted on the top shelf.

Admittedly, Aaron had a smaller stature. The top of his head only came to the shoulders of the man who decided to help him, and all that was left of the cereal he wanted was on the very top shelf, since it had sold out below. But normally he would have just stood on the bottom shelf and reached it on his own. The man had seen Aaron making preparations for the climb and walked over, towering over him and putting his hand on one of the boxes before speaking. "Did you want one of these?" he asked. And he smiled sweetly, so sweetly.

There was no point in Aaron declining his offer at that point. "If you would please."

The man brought it down, put it into Aaron's basket himself with a quick, confident movement, and then continued down the aisle. Before he rounded the corner to the next aisle, Aaron could see the man reach into his pocket and quickly glance at his Karma Card.

Those were the people that Aaron hated the most, with a sincere, unhealthy passion. The type of people that couldn't wait longer than a second to see how much their charity had earned them. While he, the supposed benefactor of their kindness, was still recovering from the embarrassment of receiving their help, from being in an inferior position to them, what concerned them most was how much it had benefitted them.

He hadn't always felt that way. He used to believe strongly in the importance of everyone helping each other, in times of need and even when there was no need at all. He enjoyed the sense of community that it brought, that everyone was there for each other, able and always willing. It had never made him feel inferior to receive help, he had felt instead like he was part of a long chain of benevolence, like he could pass forward that charity and soon it would come right back to him—there was no above and below, no inferior and superior, just a circle. And when he had felt that way, the Karma Card made sense to him. If everyone was to be directly rewarded every time they helped someone else, that was just one more good thing that it brought.

Over time that feeling had sickened, though. And he wasn't quite sure why. It was something like cynicism. There had always been an economic reason for the Karma Card, and he had always known about it, but lately he felt like it was the only reason, like the kindness and Good Works everyone had been inclined to do had never really meant anything at all. It was true that there were far too many people on the Earth, and that their consumption had to be limited somehow. With the sheer productivity of the machines that ran their lives, humanity would have consumed the entire world in a matter of years without a limit of some sort. It was the fact that the limit was chosen to be human kindness that bothered him, that kindness was turned into a job simply because ninety percent of the world would have been unemployed otherwise.

And in purely practical terms, it made sense to him. If it was the case that so many people were to be given an arbitrary, meaningless job to keep them occupied and financially restricted, then why not give them a job that ensured that they all treated each other decently. But by doing that they cheapened the value of decency, they had everyone doing it for the wrong reasons. He felt.

He stood in the frozen-food section for a while, his head in one of the freezers, just to try to remember what a real winter felt like. It smelled stale. When people began to stare—most likely considering to themselves how they could help—he decided that it was probably time to leave.

He looked at his Karma Card as he waited in line at the cashier. In the top left corner was a dollar amount, three thousand dollars. The things in his basket would lower that number to twenty-nine hundred. If he could just bring himself to pick up someone's dropped hat, the number would go up and he could buy more and keep living as he had done before, content enough to get by. But the number had only been going down for quite a while, because he couldn't bring himself to do any of it. The cashier robot scanned his items and then he left.

On the subway home he glanced around the car at all of the faces of the people onboard. There was a mother and her child, the child sitting on her lap. The child had a balloon in her hand that she kept letting go of, and an elderly man adjacent to their seat would always grab it and return it to her hand with a fatherly smile. Aaron knew that the man was just a stranger to them, that by luck he found a seat next to a child so young and was taking advantage of every moment he could. Further down an older man was smoking, looking out the window at the tunnel walls as they passed by smoothly. A great time to smoke, Aaron thought, but he couldn't afford the luxury.

Suddenly his Karma Card began to ring, and he pulled it out of his pocket. On the screen was a picture of his wife, and two buttons to either accept or ignore the call. He answered it and put the Card up to his ear. "Hello?"

"Aaron, I thought you'd be home by now. It's almost dinner time."

"I had to go to the store to get things for dinner, I told you."

"But that was hours ago, I really thought that you would have gotten back by now. I've been waiting."

"Well I'm on the subway now," he said a little impatiently while looking at the elderly man, who was currently tying the string of the balloon around the child's wrist. Apparently he'd cashed it in for everything it was worth. "I'll be home in five minutes, promise."

When he hung up the Card, he noticed that the call had

cost him three dollars. "You just keep going down, you stupid number," he said to all the wealth he had in the world, that number in the top-left corner of his Card. "Until I find a way around you."

The problem with his apathy, and his decision to let it take over, was that he had his wife Sam that depended on him at least some of the time. She easily made money at a far quicker rate than he did, but it wouldn't be enough to support two people, because no matter how charitable a person might be, the system was designed to never let anyone get too far ahead. Soon their rent would be due, and the Tax, and there would be more groceries the next day, and every phone call, every subway ride, everything everywhere was slowly draining the little money he had left.

A teenager seated across from him was playing a video game on his Karma Card, and the stern concentration on his face amused Aaron. "Are you winning?" he asked, which was very unusual for his normally shy behavior.

The teenager was reluctant to relax his focus. "This isn't the kind of game you win," he said, without breaking eye contact with his Card.

"Well what kind of game is that." Aaron noticed a patch of hair on the side of the teenager's head that was slightly shorter than the rest, and realized that the kid probably hadn't had his Card very long.

While children were still in school, usually around the age of fourteen, they were introduced into the economy all at once by inserting a chip into their head. A Karma Chip, directly connected to the neurons of the brain, which transmitted all of those random synapse firings to Karma itself, a large computer located in the middle of New York City, where the moral worth of all their actions was analyzed, assigned a dollar amount, and then transferred directly to the Karma Card of that person. Actions that were worth any amount at all were commonly referred to as Good Works. Aaron couldn't stand it.

"Would you pass me one of those newspapers there, by chance?" Aaron asked the kid, changing the subject.

"Why don't you get it yourself?" he responded, still entranced by the screen of his Card.

"How is it that you're paying for that game right now?" was Aaron's reply.

The kid hesitated momentarily, but then reached to a stack by the side of his seat and produced a newspaper, which he gave courteously to Aaron.

It always amazed Aaron that such an archaic tradition persisted so long, the printing of newspapers. It went all the way back to the sixteenth century, if he remembered correctly, and even though technology had advanced so far, they were still everywhere. Of course, they weren't made out of paper, like they used to be, but the feeling was the same. He figured that they still existed because the Government wanted people to know at least some of the news, without the fear that they were being charged for it. Either way, he enjoyed reading through them on the subway.

The first page was a large picture of a man, smiling and apparently speaking to someone that didn't quite make it into the shot. He was objectively handsome, middle aged, and seemed to talk with his hands, although the picture offered only one instant in time. Charles Darcy, the headline said. Aaron had never heard of him, and decided to take the time to read the thin column that bordered the picture.

A modern entrepreneur, it said. But not like the entrepreneurs of old, that made their money by deceiving and taking from the wealth of others, a primitive notion that had died a long time before. An entrepreneur of kindness. A man that had somehow, by sheer philanthropic willpower, raised himself into the upper class. It didn't sound possible to Aaron, the system didn't allow for it. The upper class was the sole property of the Government, and according to the article the man was just a common citizen. Yet there it was, on the front page of the official newspaper, a man of unquestionable affluence—Aaron could see it in his demeanor. How did he do it?

The full title of the article was "Charles Darcy: It Could Happen to You," but Aaron didn't understand how. The only quote from the man himself was pretty much what he expected from the kind of person the newspaper depicted Charles to be. It said, "I wasn't even aware until recently that the money I was making was more than the average person. My only concern was the betterment of my fellow man, and I will admit that I've pursued it with all of my energy. Now that I know of my wealth, I will be sure to pay it forward, as I always have with all my resources, and always will." An impossibly kind man. The rest of the article was about the peculiarity of the situation, and it also commented obliquely on the lesson that could be learned by everyone else on the matter.

"I'll keep that in mind," Aaron said to himself. "Be really, really nice to everyone. Don't even ever notice that you're making money while you're doing it. That's the key, right there."

It was only then that Aaron noticed that a pair of men,

seated several feet away from him on his left, were discussing the same article. One of them was saying how he had always known that it was possible to escape the rut of poverty, and that Charles Darcy was the proof. He said he just needed to try a little harder, but he had always known that as well. The other man was nodding and staring down the long corridor of the subway.

"My God, it's propaganda, isn't it," Aaron continued to himself. "They're giving us something stupid to believe in, so that we'll buy into the system even more, rather than rejecting it like we should. This Charles person probably doesn't even exist, it's easy enough to make up a story." He had been speaking out loud, but then decided that he'd said enough, not because he was worried about the opinion of anyone around him, but because everything he said and saw was transmitted through his Karma Chip and stored on a hard drive somewhere, where it could be used against him if anyone ever found it there. A man as obscure as he was didn't have much to worry about, but it was still best not to tempt fate by speaking poorly about the Government. So he stopped.

The subway finally reached his stop. He got up and became one with the mass of people that was let out into the basement of a station half a mile away from where he lived with his wife. Upstairs and outside he could see the diffraction pattern of the sun through the Solar Kite that extended out past all of the pollution in the atmosphere. "It's going to be one of those beautiful days, isn't it," he said. "Some sun in the sky and some dinner on the way. Just lovely."

2

WILL WATCHED INTENTLY as a child wandered back and forth along the edges of a subway platform. It was a little boy, and his mother had her back turned, gossiping all too vacuously with another woman waiting for the next train and completely oblivious to her child behind her. It was a thing of beauty, he thought to himself, it was how all parenting should be done. The kind of neglect that kept the world running. In the distance he could hear the sounds of the train on its way, and he prayed. The child was literally playing a balancing game on the concrete ledge that was four feet above the tracks below, which was about a foot taller than the kid appeared to be.

And suddenly it happened—hardly without a sound the kid fell over, arms flailing, and disappeared from view. Will looked to his right, where the train was still out of sight but loudly approaching, and kissed his cross around his neck before he stood up and ran. As he got closer to the ledge, he realized that the train was much closer than he had thought it was, so he vaulted over the ledge and turned in midair. He hoped to land directly behind the kid, where he could just pick him up and hopefully make it back onto the platform before dying.

The kid was still lying on the ground, body across the tracks, stunned and looking into the lights of the train that was only twenty feet away. Will landed awkwardly on one of the track rails, his ankle twisting slightly so that he dropped to his knees. Desperately he tried picking the kid up by a leg and a shoulder, and heaving him up onto the platform. And for the most part it worked, although he accidentally hit its head against the concrete barrier on the way up. But he did save him, after all. And before Will could do anything else, the train hit him from the side.

The next piece of consciousness he had was sitting in the back of an Emergency Helicar, two men talking over his body. His legs were a giant, searing pain that he could hardly comprehend the intensity of. It was so much pain that it became abstract, something else entirely. He waved at it.

He wasn't much aware of what they were doing, but one of the men had taken Will's Karma Card out of his pocket and put it into some kind of reader, and was saying to the other, "How much do you think it was worth, a Good Work like that? Want to place bets before I read it?"

"That's at least two thousand, no doubt about it," the other said.

"It would be quite a laugh if it wasn't in the system at all, wouldn't it? That does happen sometimes," the first man said. "You think you're doing the world the greatest favor it's ever received and it turns out you get nothing for it, that's always a laugh. I'm sure this guy would think it was funny. I'm putting my money on... two thousand and one." He then pressed a few buttons on the reader, and looked surprised at the machine's response. "A solid three thousand," he said. "I know he nearly died over it, but that's still quite a bit for one Good Work. Either way, I was closer."

"Yeah, congratulations," said the other.

The fact that Will was on an Emergency Helicar boded well for him. The people that responded to the accident had decided that it was at least possible he would be selected, otherwise they would have just sent him on another subway to the closest hospital and wished him the best. It was at least possible. In the end it was the decision of Karma and Karma alone, but he was feeling fairly confident, when he was coherent enough to feel at all. He drifted out again.

The next moment he was in a Medachine, and he could smell burning. It was working on his legs below him. Whatever it was doing, he didn't feel like burning was necessary. It seemed rather inappropriate. He realized then that there was pain in other places, that he couldn't move his right arm, and that the entire length of his back itched horribly. Outside the glass of the machine he could just barely make out several men that had tablets in their hands, all staring at him. That time it felt like sleep that he went toward.

When he finally woke up completely, he was in a white room with another man that seemed to expect that he would be conscious, because right away the man began to speak. "You have been selected by Karma to represent the World Government as an officer of the law. I'm sure you are aware of what that means for you, and with your Karma Record I assume you knew that it was bound to be the case, but as a formality I will say the rest.

"All your personal belongings are currently being moved to your new residence at 4973 West Hampshire. No need to remember the address, you'll find it on your Karma Card. All rates for Good Works of which you are the agent are henceforth to be doubled, in accord with your new position. Starting tomorrow you are to report at 6 a.m. World Time for training, which is to be completed within a month. And congratulations. The entire world could benefit from your example. You'll accept, I imagine?"

"Yes, of course." Will sat up, a deep headache immediately blooming as he moved his head. He held his hand up to his forehead and looked down at his legs below him, which felt strange. Below his knees, everything was metal. Prosthetics. They had the general shape of human legs, but they were wiring and plates and bolts, grafted unnaturally where they met the skin. He quickly averted his eyes.

"Why don't they look like legs?" he asked irritably. "Can't you put skin on them?"

"That's cosmetic," the man replied. "They're legs, not your face. If you feel that it matters that much to you, then save up some money and you can pay for it yourself, later. Until that point just wear some pants. I suppose I should mention a few things about them too, since you brought it up," he continued, indicating Will's new legs. "They may feel unusual at first. Expect to trip a few times. But in a month or two you shouldn't even notice the difference anymore." He placed a bottle of pills on a table that was between them. "Four times a day, orally. You're not going to want to miss a dose."

The next day, he woke up at five in the morning and took the first real hot shower he'd had in his entire life. Because his balance was so poor, he had to hold on to a bar that ran along the length of the shower the whole time, and still he fell once. Even then, it was an extraordinary experience for him. He never would have imagined how nice hot water could be.

Outside the bathroom, in the kitchen and his bedroom, were real appliances he'd only ever seen in stores. A refrigerator, an instant microwave, a television—it was all a dream. But he only had enough time to get himself dressed, and then slowly wobble down the hallway of the apartment complex towards the elevator at the end. He took along a walking stick that he had almost refused out of pride, back at the hospital, but was soon deeply thankful for. In his pocket was the morphine the doctor had given him, and his Card.

Even the subway was nicer, which he found to be amusing. Since it only serviced the wealthier neighborhoods, it was perhaps to be expected, just so that it would match the rest of the buildings and people. But surely a lot could be said about how well it was treated by everyone that rode on it, as the quality of person was much higher on average than all of the places that Will was used to. The women wore dresses, and the men wore suits. Government people.

The person riding across from him, a young woman, seemed to recognize his face, and smiled and whispered something into her friend's ear, sitting next to her. The other girl also turned and glanced at him quickly, but averted her eyes again when she saw that he was looking at them. "Do I know you?" he asked the first girl. "I don't really know how that could be possible. This is my first time riding this subway."

"You're Will Spector, aren't you?" she asked, somewhat shyly.

He was fairly startled. "Well yes, but… who are you?"

"Didn't you know?" she replied, and stood up to get a newspaper from the end of the row of seats. She opened it up in front of him when she returned. "Only second page, but that's pretty impressive still," she said as she laughed without much confidence. And there he was, second page of the newspaper.

The picture was a fairly strong composition, he had to admit. In the foreground was the top half of his torso, his face displayed clearly, damaged and very much unconscious but easily recognizable, as medics were taking him away from the scene. In the background, the negligent woman from the day before, tightly holding her son and crying, facing the camera. The far wall of the station could be seen as well, which made him wince, since it was the wall of the subway tunnel, on which could be seen his own blood splattered against it in an impressive mural. He wondered how it was even possible—it looked like an enormous, rotten tomato had exploded. And it was pieces of him.

It made Will laugh. All in bold caps were his name and the word hero. In the article it mentioned that, for his heroism, he was to be made an officer of the police. "That is me," he said, as he handed the paper back to the girl. "Would you like to see something else?" he asked. Both of the girls nodded slowly, unsure of what he meant. He pulled up the legs of his pants, to expose his metal lower half. "Those are new."

The girls were surprised, and visibly unsettled. "Was it really worth it?" one of them asked, the one that hadn't spoken yet.

"I really don't know yet," he responded. "But so far looks good. This subway is nice."

They laughed, and then the conversation was over. He got off at the stop indicated by his Karma Card, at a place where his training to be an officer was supposed to start. He was genuinely excited to find out what that would be like for him.

The foyer of the building was much larger than any he had seen before. Real marble ran six feet up the wall, and then the ceiling was another thirty feet above that, at least. A large number of people were going in and out the main doors, and groups were standing in front of all four of the elevators that lined the far wall as he walked in. In the center was a large fountain, in the shape of a hexagon. He followed the map on his Card, which told him to take the first elevator on his right to the ninety-third floor.

Even though he started out with a large group of people, by the time he got to his floor he was the only one left in the elevator. It was starting to make him feel nervous. It felt like a mistake—he thought that at least one person should have been going to the same place that he was. The door finally opened up into an empty, long hallway, which, following his Card, he took to the end. Then there was a staircase going down into a room, where he found three people, two wearing bullet vests and earpieces, the other wearing a suit and tie, all standing in front of a door. The one with the suit greeted him.

"Mr. Spector, pleasure to meet you. At the very least, you are prompt, and that's good to see."

"And it's a pleasure to meet you, Mr. …"

"My apologies, it's Wake. Edgar Wake."

"Pleasure to meet you, Mr. Wake." After looking around the empty room, Will added, "This isn't quite what I expected. Is this really where I will be training?"

The man laughed politely. "No, no, we like to start the first day off specially, to give you a taste of what you will be here for if you make it through training. And it really is a rare opportunity. Chances are that you might never be in this room again. You're going to talk to Karma."

"Talk to Karma? Karma is a machine, isn't it? What do you mean by that?"

"You'll find out on your own," was Edgar's reply, and he gestured to the two men that accompanied them. One of them stepped forward to address Will.

"If you'll please hand over your Card and the bottle you have in your left pocket." Will hesitated for a moment, but then set his walking stick aside and did as he was instructed. "And your shoes, please. Safety precautions." Will had to wonder what was so unsafe about his shoes, but he handed those over too. It left his robotic feet exposed, since he had decided that he was done with socks for life.

"Is that everything, then?" he asked, as he took his walking stick back in hand.

"Put that back where it was, please. You're not allowed to have it in Karma's room."

That frustrated Will, but he did as he was told. He was going to fall over in front of everyone, he was convinced. The other man opened the door they were standing in front of, and waved Will forward. He dragged his feet along the ground to keep stable, and slowly made his way in. The door was shut behind him, leaving him alone.

The room was dark, but lit in places by a startling shade of green. All the surfaces he could see were smooth and rounded, with the light emitting somewhere between where they met each other. None of it seemed necessary to his practical mind, since a single decent light bulb could have done the same amount of work, and none of the surfaces seemed to have any utility other than to be there. He proceeded forward to a small clearing that was surrounded by a circle of green.

A voice came out of the walls. "Welcome, Will Spector." It was a deep, resonating voice, one that used all of the sounds necessary to make clearly intelligible words but could never have been the voice of a human.

"Karma?" he asked.

"Of course. Do you have any questions?"

It struck him as a very strange way to start a conversation, which he attributed to the fact that it was, after all, a machine he was talking to. Strangeness aside, he wondered if he did have any questions. There before him was the machine that, in a sense, he had been serving his whole life without really knowing anything about, but nothing occurred to him to ask it. "I don't know," he finally said.

"I've been watching you for a long time, Will Spector. You've done a lot of good things. What was your intention?"

The question caught him entirely by surprise. There was surely a wrong answer to it, and he felt like the most honest answer he could give would be that wrong one. Instead, he said, "I was just doing what I was supposed to."

The machine actually laughed at his answer, Karma laughed at him. He felt ready to die. Karma said, "I can see all the things you do, and say, but I don't know what you think. You wanted to be an officer, didn't you?"

"Yes, yes I do."

"Those legs are an improvement, then," it said. It sounded like a joke, but it couldn't have been. A machine couldn't joke. "You'd give your entire body, your entire life, for the sake of what is right, wouldn't you? That is why I brought you here."

He felt like he could, so he said, "Yes."

"Then I see no reason that you shouldn't get what you want. You'll be an officer. We won't speak again, but I trust you will always know what I want. That makes it simple."

Will found a question, he just didn't know how to phrase it. He had never expected Karma to possess a consciousness, and most likely it didn't, but at that moment he couldn't tell the difference, and it was concerning him. "Why didn't I know more about you?" he finally settled on.

"You'll find that it will be the right thing to do, to never mention me to anyone, just like everyone before you found. I trust you, that is why you're here. And perhaps you don't understand the reasons now, but you will," Karma said.

"What if I decide to quit? Not to do it? What then?"

"You won't," it said. After a moment, it added, "You'll have nothing more to say. You can leave. It was nice meeting you, Will Spector. Make me proud."

Only confused, Will slowly shuffled his way out of the room. At the very least he made it through the whole ordeal standing.

3

CHARLES DARCY WAS sitting at his favorite bench in the City Park, reading a book on electrodynamics. It was late afternoon on a warm winter day, and the sky around was abysmally grey, as it always was. Not far away from where he sat was one of the pillars that connected to the Solar Kite above. The pillar had the appearance of the struggling trees around it, only it never ended, just extended until it was lost in the dark cloud in the far distance overhead. It had roots too, he knew, that branched off one by one, becoming thinner and thinner, until they were the copper wire running through every wall of every building in the city.

It had always amused him that it was the City Park they had decided to place such a pillar in, all of those practical-minded people who had designed the system all those years ago. It didn't seem like the kind of thing that belonged in a park, an electrical tower. But, as he saw it, it served as a reminder that it was still nature that provided the energy, the sun above giving its life to the trees, even if the only tree that saw the sun anymore was extremely artificial. Although, he doubted many people saw it the same way. The Solar Kite, soaring above the dark clouds of the world.

So many people had been waving at him lately, ever since he made his appearance in the newspaper. Some had even tried to strike up a conversation with him, sitting next to him on the bench and waiting for him to acknowledge them from behind his book. A lot of them asked for advice on how to be a better person, which always made him laugh internally. It still had the excitement of being novel to him, but he felt more sure by the moment that the distraction was going to be a detriment to his studies, if he chose to continue reading in the Park.

He looked up just in time to notice two officers approaching him. When he saw them, he was quick to put the book into the bag that he had underneath his seat, where they couldn't see it.

As they arrived at his bench, a young, muscular man with short facial hair didn't even wait to be acknowledged before saying, "Weren't you just reading a book?"

Charles looked up to meet his eyes, and smiled amiably. "I was, but I had intended to leave. May I help you?"

"I hope we didn't catch you at a bad time," the officer said, returning the smile. "But we were hoping to speak with you. You're a hard man to find, Mr. Darcy. I'm Eric Devlin." He extended a hand to shake. Charles took it, to avoid seeming rude. "And this is Marcus Cole. May we sit down?"

"By all means. And I can't be that hard to find. You have your fancy machines."

Eric was the kind of person that relentlessly carried the conversation forward at his own pace, which often made him dismissive. "Very true. Speaking of that, this is an interesting place for a man like you to be, Mr. Darcy. A Privacy Room. You are aware that nothing you do here counts, aren't you?"

"I find it offensive that you refer to this place as a Room," he answered.

"It's just a technical term."

"I know it is," Charles said, a little too shortly. Eric had his legs splayed out in front of him, and his arms around the back of the bench, as if he was entirely at leisure. And maybe he was.

"I would have expected you to be more polite, after reading all about you," Eric said. The man named Marcus had yet to speak, and seemed like he never would. He had a large, firm jaw, and eyes that were set far deeper than the average person, which made his face a strange combination of stern and comical. He just stared off into the distance, at the people walking through the Park.

"And I would have expected the same from a police officer, but then again I've only read about them as well," Charles said.

Eric laughed heartily. "Only read about? Never met an officer before. Now I can hardly believe that." And he laughed again. "I'm sorry," he continued, "somehow this turned into a casual conversation that it was never meant to be. I'll get to the point. I'm here to tell you that you've been selected by Karma to be a member of the Government. Which I'm sure you've expected."

"And what position am I being offered?"

"Something administrative. I don't know many of the details, but something entirely suited to your character, rest assured."

"As you said," Charles replied, "I had expected. But I would like to respectfully decline."

Eric lost his cheery attitude very quickly. He stumbled to say, "Were you hoping for a different kind of position? I don't understand. Whatever it is, I'm sure it can be resolved, but you'll have to come with us."

"It has nothing to do with the type of position," he said. "If it is the Government, I don't want to be involved. And I won't be going with you."

"Given your circumstances, it's not possible to refuse."

"That can't be true."

"Well, why would you? I know you already found your way into money, but think of how much more—"

Charles interrupted him without consciously intending to. "It has nothing to do with the money, I will say that much. Now really I must be going," he said, standing up and taking his bag from under the bench.

Eric frowned. "We'll be in touch."

"Great."

After a long subway ride, Charles stood in front of his mansion in Champlain. It was an archaic building that had been abandoned until only two weeks before, when he had bought it and made his public appearance as a man that had more money than he should. Directly behind it was the former country of Canada, which for reasons of habit was still considered by most to be foreign.

He went straight through the large living room, down one of the three hallways, and into the bathroom on its left. There was no mirror on the wall. He spoke loudly into the sink. "Brother Vincent, send Brother Peril over here right away. And activate the exchange."

"Right away," came a voice from his sink. Instantly a portion of the tiled floor lifted up, exposing a complicated set of machines with two seats and a control panel. He didn't have to wait long before another man knocked on the door.

"How many times do I have to tell you that you don't have to knock?" Charles said through the door.

Peril opened it and walked in. "It's always weird. It is a bathroom after all."

Charles was already seated in one of the chairs of the machine. "Sit down, please. We don't have much time."

As soon as Peril was seated, Charles hit a few buttons and the machine began to move as it hummed. It removed the ears of both men, took a Karma Chip out of Charles' head, and put it into Peril's. The whole time, both men had a very pained look on their face. When their ears were replaced, Charles stood up and said to Peril, "I think I'm close to figuring out the Karma Chip. And then we can abandon this godforsaken machine. But it really is complicated, and I might never make it in time for it to matter."

Peril was absentmindedly holding on to his ear as he just nodded slowly.

Charles said, "You're going to have to stop doing that. Stop touching your ear. Thank you. I want you to stay here for maybe an hour or two, perhaps watch some television, and then go back into the city." He handed Peril his own Karma Card. "It's going to be harder from here on out. The police talked to me today. If you notice that they're around you, it's probably because they're looking for me. I imagine you'll be safe, even when they know exactly where you are, because I doubt they'll be able to make sense out of any of it. But if you do have trouble, call the house phone."

"You really don't think they'll suspect anything if you call yourself when you live alone?"

"I said if you're in trouble. I'm leaving." Charles left the bathroom, going to the back of his house and out the door, into his expansive backyard. He hopped a small fence, then cut between a few trees and a thick brush, and found himself in the middle of a small town.

He called it the Monastery, the land of the dead. There were one hundred tents and counting, which represented two hundred monks. Further along the path he walked there was a moderately sized farm, where they grew everything that they could possibly grow, and even further down was where they kept their animals. Even though he had only publicly owned the mansion for two weeks, the Monastery had been there for about two years, and it was his pride and joy. There was even a small, wooden temple where he occasionally gave a sermon on Sundays. It was the temple that he was on his way to.

Situated in the back of the temple was the only room that was undeniably modern, which he had to include as a necessity. It housed monitors, computers, radios, and a workbench littered with countless tools and spare parts. Three people were standing at the bench, hard at work on small machines he had them building. He took a few books from his bag, including the one on electrodynamics, laid them on the bench, and said to them, "Required reading, for all of you."

He then found Vincent, seated in a chair in front of the monitors.

"How is everyone doing?" he asked Vincent.

"Have a look for yourself," he said, and turned one of the screens towards them. It was a map of New York City, with one hundred dots spread out all across it. Each one represented one of his monks, out in the city, doing Good Works so that his enterprise could have the money it needed to carry out its mission.

"And they're all alright?"

"All of the vitals are normal."

"Who is that?" Charles asked, pointing to a circular monitor off to the side.

"That's Brother Michael. He's been opening the door for people at the Century Building all day." On the screen was the visual perspective of Michael, as he stood outside the door of a building, facing the busy street. Thousands of people were walking by, and whenever one diverted into the building, he could be seen moving aside and letting them in.

Michael was one of the newer members of the Order, and Charles made sure that they were monitored for at least a week's worth of duty, before he sent out another new member for training. Vincent was one of the four people that were always in the monitor room, watching the new recruits.

"And how much longer does he have to be watched?"

"Today's his last day. He did fine. Simple, but fine," Vincent said.

"That's good enough. Where's the next one?"

"Should be in the temple today. His name is Steve."

"Alive or Dead?"

"Dead."

"Thank you, Brother Vincent."

"An honor, Brother Charles."

Around the other side of the building were the large wooden doors of the temple. During the day, they were open. On the inside, fifty monks were sitting on the ground in lotus position, meditating. All except one of them were wearing black robes—the exception was wearing white. Charles walked through the rows and columns of people until he stood in front of him. "Steve," he said. When he got no response, he lightly rapped on the man's head with his finger. "Steve?"

The man woke with a startle, and when he recognized the face of the man standing above him he tried getting to his feet as quickly as he could, so that he could bow or display some sort of etiquette. "Sir, my mistake, sir."

"Stay seated," he said, as he sat down on the floor himself. "And please, call me Brother Charles. There are no 'sirs' here."

"Yes, Brother Charles."

"Before I say anything else, pull in your legs a little, for a better lotus. Your chi is entirely off-balance. You'll never find Enlightenment with your legs sticking that far out."

He waited for the man to correct his posture, then continued. "Now as I understand it, it will be tomorrow that you actually go into the world as a Brother of our Order and do Good Works in our service." The man just sat there in silence listening, which Charles appreciated. "There are a few things we haven't told you about yet, and now is the time. After this conversation, I will give you your black robes, so if you need to hear again any of the things I will be saying, you can ask any other Brother and they will know that they can tell you.

"You are Dead. That means that the Karma Chip we took out of your head, two months ago when you got here, was destroyed. And your death was fabricated. As far as the world is concerned, you no longer exist. Half of the Brothers you see around you are still Alive. Their Chip is still out there, being used. But not necessarily by them. Only half of the time. You will be paired with someone that is Alive, and you will be them for half of their remaining life, as far as Karma is concerned.

"It is important that you get to know the Brother you are paired with fairly well. There will be a file put into your tent for you to read tonight, make sure you read it thoroughly. It's important that the actions you do are not too out of character with respect to the person who you will become. It is important that you never look into a mirror, if possible. And in general, avoid reflective surfaces and suspicious behavior.

"There are twenty bathrooms that we control, positioned across New York City, where you will switch with your partner. It involves that machine with the ear thing, and I apologize in advance. They are all located in restaurants that we are affiliated with, where you yourself will be eating every other night, although the cumulative effect will be that the identity you share with your partner will eat there every night. You may see Brothers you recognize on the streets, and especially at these restaurants. It is important that you don't ever acknowledge them.

"You will be doing Good Works for the whole day, on days that you are in the city. A good work ethic will be expected of you. A large portion of your earnings has already been arranged to be deducted from the Karma Card you share, as a monthly bill, so don't be surprised when you see that deduction. You will be monitored for a week's worth of duty, which will take two week's time. Days that you are here will be divided exactly the same way as you're used to. Half of the time you will be on the farm, half of the time you will be meditating here. The only difference is that your cycle will now consist of three days instead of two."

Charles took a moment to study the reaction on the man's face, to see if he could sense any hesitation or misgiving. He was mostly satisfied with what he saw there. "Do you have any questions, at the moment?"

"No, I don't believe I do."

"Then welcome to the Order, Brother Steve."

4

SPREAD OUT ON a table in front of Will were some of the most exciting things that he had ever seen in his life. Nothing in his new apartment compared. A man was seated on the opposite side of the table, and was explaining each of them one by one.

"Chances are you've only ever seen a few of these before, because that's how it was for most of us when we first started, so I'll take you through them one at a time. These you've seen before," he said as he picked up a bundle of triangular shaped objects. "This is a Privacy Room, and there should be eight pieces in there. You get one extra Room, and it's yours to put wherever you want."

"I don't know what I would do with it," Will said.

"Some people like to do weird stuff in their kitchen. Just hold on to it, you'll think of something. But you can't give it away. They're pretty easy to use, you just pull these tabs and stick them wherever you want. But make sure you get it right the first time, because they take literally a second to set and then you can't move them."

A Privacy Room was a small area defined by those triangles, inside of which a Karma Chip didn't transmit data to Karma. Every citizen that owned a house or apartment was allowed to have at most two Rooms, one for their bathroom and one for their bedroom. Businesses were strictly limited in a similar way, although the rule wasn't as simple. Most every other public place was monitored by Karma, with the exception of the City Park, which was the only Privacy Room that was as large as it was. Early in the implementation of Karma, it had been decided that at least some privacy should exist for the people that it monitored, since all of the things that it recorded—everything that a person saw or heard—could easily be looked up by quite a large number of people that had the authority to do so. The Park had been a similar concession to public privacy. The assumption had been that there wouldn't be that many Good Works being done in bedrooms and bathrooms anyway, so there wouldn't be many people complaining about lost opportunities to make money.

"These are high-torsion handcuffs, only for people you hate. If you try to get out of them at all, they start twisting. The more you struggle, the more they twist. I saw a man once that tried to get out of them, ripped his arms clean off. Funny but disgusting, so be careful. These over here are normal handcuffs, as you can see they do look slightly different, so try to remember the difference. This is a Grappling Chain, just shoot it at a wall and then you have a slightly elastic bond between you and that wall. It's elastic so that your arms don't get ripped off. I'm not saying you will get pushed off of a building, but if you do you'll be glad you have this, and you'll be glad it doesn't rip your arms off too. They have a practice course for it that you'll be going through, but if you're feeling really brave you can try it whenever you want.

"These are steroids that you now have a prescription for. Among other things, like muscle strength and reflex speed, they also strengthen your tendons and joints, particularly the shoulder socket. So that it's harder to rip your arms off.

"A lock gun. This is a stun gun, temporarily paralyzes the central nervous system. A lot of guns. This is an Evaporation Pen, you can have it now but it won't be activated until you're done with your training, and only then when Karma allows it. Have you ever seen one of these used?"

Will shook his head.

"Well nothing I could say would prepare you for it. This is the range selector right here, but unless you have special permission five feet is all you get. You point this end right here at a person, press this button, and then they don't exist anymore. Not even their arms. And they're not teleporting, or shrinking really small, or any other thing that would make you feel alright about pressing the button. They turn instantly into a gas. You'll actually feel the breeze from the increase in pressure they create, if you're standing close enough. It's mostly just carbon dioxide and water vapor, but a little bit of carbon monoxide can't be helped so it's best if you just hold your breath when you do it. Here's that for you.

"These shoes are awesome, but I'm not even going to explain them to you. It'll be a nice little surprise whenever you figure it out. Good luck with that. These are Identity Mines, explosives that work when the person they're identified for walks by. You'll have to wait for those to work too. Benefits that you don't see on the table in front of you are the house you live in and your Good Work rate increase, as I assume you're aware of. You'll find also that transportation, phone calls, and certain restaurants marked on your Karma Card are all free now.

"And I'm sure that all of that sounds pretty cool to you, but

I saved what I think is the best for last, like I always do when I'm giving the speech," he said as he pulled out a small disc-shaped object. "I don't even know why I think it's the best. In a lot of ways it's the least exciting of any of these, but I think you'll find that it's the one that will keep you up late at night just thinking." He laid it out in front of them and put his finger down in its center. It switched on, only to reveal a map of New York City seen from above.

"The Karma Map. This is literally the collective conscious of the world. It's the most up-to-date map possible, because it's a compilation of what everyone everywhere is seeing. You can zoom in and out. You can go to other continents too if you want, but only if you're going sightseeing. These little dots," he said as he zoomed in, "you just tap on one." And when he did, it became the viewpoint of a person as they walked down a busy street. A man held a door open as they entered a building. The sounds of the crowd could be heard faintly emanating from the disc. "Suddenly you're that person. If you can find a person, you can follow them around. Or if you know their Karma Card information, you can also just enter that in.

"You can also…" he said as he touched something else on the disc. "Yeah, look at this." It was the map of the city, like before, only there was a bright path cutting across all of it like a tunnel. "This is everywhere that person has been in the last twenty-four hours. You can go back a lot further, but it gets kind of confusing if they've been around a lot. If you have a suspicion that the person standing in front of you just shot a man a couple hours ago, you do all of this and suddenly you can see exactly what he saw as he did it, if he did it, all displayed on this map so you know where it happened. It can be really useful like that, but it can also mess with your head. Try not to spend too much time with it. And I'm serious about that.

"The blank spots will drive you crazy. You'll ask yourself, 'why hasn't anyone ever looked here? It's right in the middle of the city.' And you'll go there and find out that it's right next to the smelliest dumpster you've ever smelled, and the most probable explanation is that everyone who walked by would probably have to turn their senses off to survive it. Something as stupid as that, but it bothered you for a whole week until you just had to go see it for yourself. Or you'll see this woman that you think is beautiful, and you'll want to spend the next two months seeing the world through her eyes. What you don't realize now is that you aren't prepared for the amount of harassment that a typical beautiful woman can go through in two months, just walking down the street, and also you'll have to remember that someone is also watching you, and you'll get in trouble if you get too far off track. And you don't want to get in trouble, I promise you. Do you have any questions?"

"Where do I put it all?"

"I'll get you a bag. But you should totally put these shoes on right now. Throw those away."

Will was no longer handled individually. After a few days of waiting around and getting to know the officers, he was put into a class of twenty other trainees, and instructed in a room by a slightly overweight but still physically impressive, heavily balding, middle-aged man by the name of Lieutenant Caplan. They had already learned and been tested on the various laws they were to be enforcing, but the lesson that day seemed to be focusing on practical concerns that would be encountered while they were working.

Lieutenant Caplan was saying, "Half of the calls that you are going to get involve someone taking too long in their bathroom. This is flagged automatically by Karma, and then you get sent to investigate because we can't see what's going on in there. You'll show up, and there will by a dead guy sitting on the toilet, half of his skull sawed off by his own hands, blood everywhere. It isn't pretty. Sometimes they'll be alive still. They think they can take the Karma Chip out themselves, without anyone knowing, with the kind of tools you can buy at a local convenience store. It never works out. What you're going to do, whether they are dead or alive still, is stand outside the bathroom, so Karma can see it, and you're going to Evaporate them. Some of you will be tempted to call an ambulance if you find one that's still moving, but I promise you that more often than not they're beyond repair, and even if they're not they've committed a felony crime, the punishment for which is death.

"Other times you'll just be doing an inspection to make sure all of their appliances are in accordance with the law. If you see anything suspicious looking, like someone attempting to modify or change their Privacy Room in any way, you are authorized to arrest them immediately. If they attack you, you are authorized to Evaporate them. But remember, Karma is always watching, so don't go around Evaporating just everyone you see. The law must be broken first.

"Another common thing you'll be doing, especially this time of year, is reminding people that the Tax is on the way, if they aren't quite ready for it. Most of these people you'll usually find at the bars, which is kind of funny in a sad way. And then after the Tax, you'll be escorting a lot of people to Rehabilitation, which can often be a messy business. We'll explain more of those details later, when we visit one of the clinics.

"Very rarely, you will be called to a scene where someone is acting violently, whether they are just disturbing the peace or actually killing other people. These are to be handled contextually. If you can make the arrest, that is preferable. But if that doesn't seem possible without risking your own livelihood, you are authorized to Evaporate them. Always, in all cases, Evaporations should be done outside of a Privacy Room. If you ever Evaporate a person while you are inside a Privacy Room, you will immediately be under investigation and all your weapons deactivated. Pressing the button creates a high-frequency signal that is detectable to Karma even inside of a Room.

"You may not Evaporate anyone in the Government, even if they are acting violently, or threatening your life. Your weapons will be deactivated immediately, if you do that. Instead, in such a case, you are required to use your stun gun and make an arrest. For every person that you arrest, you have the option of riding the subway system, or calling a Helicar to pick you up.

"And now we'll move on to the next topic," he said.

One month later, and Will was a certified officer. There was nothing ceremonious about it, no celebration, it was just that the next day he was allowed to go out into the city, carrying all of his new equipment. He was assigned to another officer, a man by the name of Eric Devlin. Eric had been an officer for only a few years, but was already well distinguished. Will was told that, for the most part, Eric would only be there to watch him perform, and that he was really on his own.

On his Karma Card was a list of numbers that he was to visit in sequential order. There was no explanation that went along with any of them. When he tapped on the first one, a marker popped up on his Map, on the thirty second floor of some building three miles away. He and Eric took a quick sub-way ride, and then an elevator, and then Will was standing at the door of his first official business as a police officer.

He had never been in such an unsightly building before. Nearly all of the lights that lined the hallway were flickering, and patches of the carpet were missing everywhere. He could have sworn he saw a rat, which had supposedly been extinct for ten years. He knocked politely on the door. At his side, Eric laughed.

"Why are you laughing?" Will asked, a little too irritably.

"Do you really think he's going to answer?" was all he said in reply.

Will hesitated momentarily, but then tried turning the han-dle. It was locked. He patiently opened his duffle bag, found his lock gun, and put it against the door knob. When he pulled the trigger, it made a high-pitched whirring sound and pushed the door open a few inches. Before he entered, he peered in through the slit of the door to see if he could make anything out. All he could see were dirty clothes and a large brown stain on the far wall.

"Here, let me get that for you," Eric said, and pushed the door open all the way. A horrendous smell suddenly reached Will from the breeze created by the door opening, and he staggered back a few feet to the opposite end of the hallway. "You're going to have to have a stronger stomach than that," Eric said, standing unaffected in the threshold. "And be quick-er."

Will regained his composure, brought out his Evaporation Pen, and walked into the room. There was a small, overflowing kitchen to the left, and a short hallway to the right that had two doorways. One would be the bedroom, the other the bathroom. He was sure, from the smell, that he would find a rotting corpse behind at least one of those doors. First he opened the bedroom, and didn't see anything besides a deeply sagging bed with formerly white sheets, unmade. The Privacy Room triangles could be seen in the corners, surrounded by peeling wallpaper. He closed the door again.

"The bathroom," Will said. He had his eyes half-closed when he opened the door, expecting to not want to see whatever it was. And there was a lot of blood, all over the floor, and the wall, and in the sink. But the man that was propped up in the shower, the spring of all that blood, was still moving, and looked up at him when he entered. The bathroom was too small for Eric to fit in, he just stood outside and watched.

"Oh good, you came," the man said slowly, slurring his words. There were several empty bottles of alcohol scattered along the ground in the blood, Will saw. "Could you help me? I almost got it." The man swallowed heavily, and a fresh stream of blood left his exposed skull. "It's deep, real deep."

Will looked back at Eric. Eric made a silent gesture for him to turn back around. "Sir, what you've done is a felony," Will said in an official tone. "I'm going to Evaporate you now."

"Do you think I don't know that?" he said. "Do you think I don't know that? I know that."

Will's hand trembled heavily as he held up the small Pen, pointed at the man. He had to be within five feet, that's what the range selector said. He had to hold his breath. Carbon monoxide, he would feel really tired and then he wouldn't feel anything at all. "You knew the consequences," he said quietly, weakly.

"Back out of the bathroom," Eric said, when he thought that Will might push the button from inside. "Your head has to be behind the doorway. Back up."

Will nearly tripped on his new legs, since he wasn't used to walking backwards in them yet, and he didn't turn around to do what Eric said, he just moved.

"That's good. Turn on the fan."

Will fumbled for the switch with his left hand, his right one still pointing the Pen at the man that was incoherently muttering something to his shower faucet. "Goodbye," he said, and pressed the button.

He shouldn't have watched it happen, although he felt like he should, felt like it would be better for him if he desensitized himself to it as soon as possible. But he shouldn't have watched it happen. The Pen emitted a bright red beam that hit the man on the right side of his chest. Radiating from that point, he became a cloud, which engulfed his entire body in the space of a second. And Will could feel it, the wind that followed. He dropped his Pen and threw up violently.

"That was really good," Eric said. "You'll do really great. Now pick your Pen back up."

5

CHARLES DARCY WAS sitting in a firm leather chair in a dressing room, waiting to be interviewed on national television. He was in the Television City Tower, the headquarters of one of the few major news broadcasters not yet owned by the Government.

Although Top World News was as popular as it was, he was worried that it might be suspicious that it was the only interview he had agreed to, even though agents of many of the other, Government-owned news stations had been calling him constantly ever since he'd rejected a Government position. Top World News was not openly anti-Government, because if it was it wouldn't have existed, but it did have certain associations that he wanted to distance himself from, while at the same time taking advantage of the public platform that their interview provided him. He had to think carefully about how to present his case, very carefully.

He was extremely tired, but couldn't allow the world to notice. He had been forced to be himself nearly all of the past week, and had been finding it extremely difficult. He had an image to preserve, while at the same time a secret that would cost him and his entire Order their lives, if it was discovered.

A man knocked on the door. Without waiting for a response, a voice said, "Mr. Darcy, they're ready for you outside."

He stood up slowly, smoothed his tuxedo out with his hands, and left the room. He found himself in a brightly lit hallway. There was a short man wearing an earpiece, standing at the far end, that waved him over. When he got there, the man said, "You'll walk through this door, Mr. Darcy, and turn left. You can wave at the studio audience if you want. You will sit down in the chair closest to you, facing Mr. Spencer. There will be a glass of water underneath the chair, on the left, if you find yourself getting thirsty. The lights are really bright, I must warn you." The man stopped talking, and inclined his head slightly, as if he was listening to something he could hear only distantly. "Okay, you're going on now. Good luck."

On the other side of the door, the lights were incredibly bright. Blindly, he waved in the direction of the audience, and they applauded loudly. Across the stage was Ryan Spencer, a famous news personality. He was standing, with his hand extended as Charles approached. They shook, and then sat down.

"Ladies and Gentlemen, Mr. Charles Darcy. You've had an extremely busy past few years, if what I hear is true. We're glad that you could make time for us," he said with a smile.

"I'm only as busy as I want to be," Charles said, trying to be modest. "And I'm glad to be here."

"For those of you that don't know his story, Mr. Darcy has been the most productive member of our society since the beginning of Karma. Five hundred Good Works a day. Twenty four hours a day—you don't sleep, Mr. Darcy. That's not an exaggeration, that's a fact learned from looking at your Record, and I would say that it wasn't physically possible if I didn't have you sitting here before me, living proof. How do you do it? And why, what motivates you? Your newspaper article made it seem like you didn't even realize that what you were doing was far from ordinary."

"I might have given the wrong impression, to the newspaper. I have known all along that I do more Good Works than all of the people that I know of, which if I'm being honest with myself means that I'm making more money. But I would have figured that, in this very large world we live on, there would be at least a few more people like me out there. To have done something unprecedented in a world this large seems nearly impossible to me, conceptually, and it still does."

Ryan moved at the speed of entertainment, from one question to the next. "You've been called a modern entrepreneur, and have been touted by the Government itself as the role model of the century. Now, I don't mean to be critical here, since there is the naked fact that the rate at which you have done Good Works is simply miraculous, but this thing about you never sleeping seems almost unfair, at least with respect to you being a role model. Do you really think people should follow your example? And are you taking some sort of medicinal supplement, to help you with what you're doing?"

His heart was racing. What scared him most about Karma was that it recorded his vitals, his blood pressure and his heart rate. He hoped that the excitement of being on national television would be enough to fool Karma, as he danced around the lies he would be telling.

"There is no doubt in my mind that in a world like ours, technologically saturated but scarce in resources, what is most important is strength in community, helping out your fellow brother. Actually, in any world, I would say that that was most important. But in the past, there were plenty of less direct

ways of doing that, a person could do research, solve problems, help advance human understanding and make the world
better that way. But that's been nearly pushed to its limit. We
have the Solar Kite, and the factories, and Karma. It's been
taken care of for us. What remains is to be kind, charitable,
and to always help when the opportunity presents itself.

"I don't take a medicinal supplement, as you called it. There
are plenty out there, and people should feel free to use them,
but I have always believed in a natural human diet, as vague as
that might sound. I don't know why I don't sleep, and I don't
recommend it to anybody. It can be scary sometimes. But
since I'm awake, and it helps to take my mind off of things,
I'm out there every day doing Good Works, which I recommend to anybody."

Ryan nodded thoughtfully, and then started in with another prompt. "There's also this matter about you turning down
a Government position. To me, that almost seems even more
unusual than your work ethic. Do you have more to say on
that?"

That point was the one Charles had to be the most careful
with. If he said the wrong things, it would be the end of everything. What was interesting about Ryan was that even though
he was famous, he did not have a large financial wealth. If he
did, he would have been forced into the Government.

Certain jobs, like the delivery of the news, couldn't be assigned to robots. There were still bartenders, waiters, pilots,
newscasters. Unless they worked for the Government, their
job was treated as a Good Work, which didn't provide them
with much more financial power than the average citizen.

Ryan was walking the fine, distinct line between popularity and citizenship. The transition to financial wealth would be impossible for him, unless he took a Government position, which almost without a doubt had been offered to him before, and was still possible for him at any time.

So there were reasons that Ryan had made the same decision that Charles had, reasons that he persisted in poverty, even when he had fame. There was a hidden question in what Ryan asked him—he was being disingenuous. Ryan didn't really think it was that unusual that Charles had declined the position. He just wanted to know why. It must have been a personal interest, since he doubted that Ryan cared for the audience at all, at that moment. What was truly unprecedented and interesting about Charles was that he was both rich and a citizen, not his work ethic.

"I have nothing to offer the Government. It's as simple as that. What I do, and who I am, only has a place as a citizen. And that is not intended as an offense to the Government, not at all. What they do is a necessity. But I don't belong behind a desk, legislating. And I'm not a politician, I don't belong on television. That is why I have only agreed to this one interview. My skills are just different."

Ryan laughed. "You're being very modest, television seems to suit you fine. Well I will thank you for being here. You really are a popular man. Whether you agree to another interview or not, I imagine you will be making the news for some time to come. It's been an honor," he said, and stood again, offered his hand again. The audience began to clap loudly. He leaned in and said, "The microphones are off. I know it's a lot to ask, but would you mind talking privately after the show? There are other things I would like to ask you."

"Of course," Charles said, and dropped the other's hand. He turned and waved at the audience again, and bowed, and was greeted by very loud cheers. With that, he left the stage.

He was directed to a room, where he waited twenty minutes for Ryan to arrive. He couldn't help but notice the triangles in the corner of the room that indicated that it was a Privacy Room. He drank a glass of water and reflected on how his first and perhaps only television appearance had gone. "They will like me or they won't," he thought to himself.

When Ryan did arrive, he poured himself a drink before he said anything at all. "Would you like one as well?" he asked, when he had finished preparing his own.

"I'm fine with water," Charles said.

"Tell me what you wouldn't tell me out there," Ryan said, without any attempt to be subtle. "And don't worry, this is a Privacy Room." He pointed at one of the corners, with the index finger of the hand that he was holding his glass with.

Charles didn't trust any Privacy Room that was not his own. And he didn't entirely trust those, half of the time. The only time he felt safe to think his own thoughts, even, was when the Chip was out of his head, a luxury that no one outside of his Order had, as far as he was aware.

It was possible that Ryan was actually an agent of the Government, who lured potential radicals into a false sense of security, only to turn them over when they admitted to their treasonous thoughts. He was firmly resolved to play innocent to the end, even though part of him thought that Ryan would have been a good ally to have, if he was real. "I get the feeling that you expect something far deeper from me than there really is. I've said everything, and there isn't anything more to it."

"I don't believe that," Ryan said. "I don't believe a damn bit of it."

"That's unfortunate," was Charles' simple reply.

"I can't let you go that easily. There is no reason why you wouldn't want to work for the Government, unless you had something to hide. Whatever fortune you have now, however you got it, would double. And you wouldn't even have to try. And you would have the option of being one of the first people to go to Mars. Now who wouldn't want that? I hear the sky is already blue. Can you imagine, a blue sky? It's a fairy tale, and you won't be able to live it unless you become one of them."

In five years, Mars would be ready to live on. They had begun terraforming it ten years before, and already they were putting in a frictionless transportation system underground, and the foundations for the skyscrapers they would build in time. Members of the Government were given an option to move there first. Most of the population of Earth wouldn't ever be given that option.

Charles chose to be aggressive, even as he played innocent. Perhaps it was a dangerous move. "I could ask you the same thing. You have all the same options, don't you? What is it that you're hiding, then? If we're using your logic."

Ryan smiled cunningly. "Well, now I don't know how much I should say, Charles. I had thought I found a friend, but perhaps I was wrong. I will say, that if you are doing what I think you are doing, I don't believe that you will get very far. This world wasn't made to be opposed. It is much larger and stronger than you, it will destroy you long before you even scratch it. I used to think that I could challenge it, but that was a long time ago."

Charles just smiled as fake as he could, and sipped his water.

"Of course," Ryan continued, "that wouldn't make sense to someone with as pure of intentions as you have. Whatever it is you're doing, I wish you the best of luck. Show the world just how much love you have to offer it, that will always do the trick."

"There's something we can agree on," Charles said.

It took three different subways to get from the studio to his mansion. On the first subway, he noticed that everyone there was looking at him, but nobody said a thing. At the first stop, when a few people left and a few more got on, a drunk man that must have just left a bar loudly announced Charles' presence to the whole car. "This guy was just on television. I was just watchin' it, I really just was. At the…" his words trailed off. "At the bar," he finished. "Nice to meet ya, good sir," he said as he stuck his dirty hand out for Charles to shake.

Charles took it firmly. So many handshakes lately, he thought. He could feel the man's weakness through his hand.

"I still have a question though," the man continued. "Why you doin' it?"

"Why am I doing what?"

"Why you bein' a saint, or whatever it is?"

"Not a saint. A citizen. I answered that already. On the television," Charles said, patiently. Everyone around was listening.

"No you didn't. I was listenin'. I was waitin' specifically to hear that answer. And I never heard it."

"I said that we're a community. And that we have to look out for each other."

"That's not a why, that's a what. Or should, or you know what I mean. 'Have to look out for each other,' you say. Well there's a lot of things that I have to do that I just don't, you know? Karma forgive me. You didn't convince me. I wanted to be convinced. They keep callin' you a hero, and I want to know why I should feel the same."

Suddenly it felt to Charles that what he said then would be just as important as what he had been trying to say on the television. If he redeemed his failure to make his point thoroughly on television, right there on a moving subway, would it spread? He didn't know. But he thought he should try. The reason that the Government called him a hero, for the moment, was because he was doing exactly what they wanted him to, he was embracing their system more firmly than they could ever hope, at least from their perspective. But that didn't appeal to the oppressed.

Karma won't like this, he thought, before he began. But he said it anyway. "I'm not doing any of the things I'm doing because it's what Karma wants," he said, and the atmosphere immediately became more intense. All that could be heard, before he spoke again, was the rattling of the subway on its tracks. *On Mars they'll be frictionless*, he thought. "It has never had anything to do with appeasing Karma. What I really want is to help. I see everyone struggling, and I want to help. That is a 'what,' but I feel like the 'why' should be obvious." He didn't have to lie, but he couldn't say the whole truth. "I think I can help us out. If we work together."

"And how do we do that?" the drunk man said, still persistent.

"I'll show you, if you can wait."

The drunk man looked at him crossly, appraising him. "Wait he says. How many people are tired of waiting?" He looked around him. Absolutely no one responded, even though all of them were listening, and thinking. "Fine," he said. "We'll wait. Good idea."

6

AARON WAS SITTING at his dinner table, discussing his finances with his wife, Sam. Not because he had wanted to, but because she was concerned with the coming rent, and then with the yearly Tax shortly after that, and she had insisted that they should make a plan.

"How are we going to split the rent this time? Can you afford half? Give me your Karma Card, I want to see it." She was still young, but lines were developing prematurely around her eyes and at the corners of her mouth. Her eyes were large relative to her face, giving them an intense, penetrating look, which she was attempting then to use to her advantage. They were entirely unsupported by her thin, fragile body, which didn't possess a single ounce of physical intimidation, but she had a deep reserve of anger that she could always resort to when she wanted to win.

"I'm not giving you my Card. I will pay half, like I always have. There's no reason I shouldn't," Aaron said.

"But how much does that leave you for the Tax? I know you haven't been earning that much lately, you can't hide that from me. You'll have two thousand, three weeks from now? You will?"

"I'm making money just fine. Don't tell me I'm not. This lack of belief in me I'm getting from you is insulting, really.

I go out there and I do exactly what I'm supposed to. It will work out. I'm paying half of the rent, and I'm paying my Tax. That's final, so stop bothering me about it, already."

"Damn it, Aaron please stop lying to me," she said as she started crying, tears eroding the intimidation in her eyes. "I know exactly how much money you have. I know the exact number. And I know that we're in trouble if you don't change. I just wanted you to admit it on your own. Please, please just admit it."

"What do you mean you know exactly how much money I have?"

"I mean I looked at your Card."

"When?"

"Yesterday. You left it on the table."

Aaron was trying to stifle a violent outburst, but his anger was making it hard. "I told you, I told you never to look at my Card. I don't care where I left it. I told you not to."

"Well it's a good thing I did, because we have a problem. Aaron, it's not just you it affects when you can't pay the Tax, and they take you away. I'm not trying to sound selfish," she said, tears streaming, "or maybe I am, it doesn't really matter. Maybe I am selfish. But if they take you away, it affects me too. I'll have to move out of this apartment we worked so hard to get, back into some ghetto. And not just that, but I love you. We have a life here together. They take you away and what happens to that? I don't know, I just don't know, but we really have to fix this, and I need you to want the same things. Because even if I make enough money to pay the rent by myself somehow, I still can't pay your Tax for you, even if I wanted to." Then she descended into uncontrollable sobbing.

Aaron really was sorry. He was placing a far larger strain on her than she deserved, and he knew it. But he was angry as well. Not necessarily at her, and her invasion of his privacy—they were married, after all. He was mad at the system, he was mad at his own lack of desire to help himself, which fell on her. More than anything he wanted to yell at her and walk away, but she was horribly pathetic, curled into a tight ball in her chair, head on the table, crying. "Just let it go. Let it happen," he said. He wanted her to feel his apathy, to know all of the reasons he had given up, without having to explain them to her.

"No, no," she said, as she somewhat regained herself, sitting back upright in her chair. "I'm not letting go. I talked to Karl. I asked him to help, I mean. He said he would. If this conversation had gone how I wanted, I was going to say you should go talk to him, and that he would take you down to the church, right away. But I asked him if he would come over here if it didn't go well." Karl was their neighbor next door, and had been since they moved in a year prior.

"What? What!" Aaron yelled, only angry by that point. "When do you think that's going to happen? And when did you plan this?"

There was a knock at their door. Still in a rage, Aaron jumped out of his chair, and flung it open. Karl was standing outside, a slow, torpid expression on his face.

"And how the hell did you plan all of this so perfectly, huh? How did you know that now would be the perfect time to come right on over and show me how to be kind to the world, huh?"

"I can hear you through the walls," Karl said.

In the elevator, Aaron had calmed down somewhat. The floors flew by. Karl had always been a good counterpoint to his own temperamental nature, and he knew that. Karl was a heavily-built, longsuffering man, and he stood silently next to Aaron as they descended.

"I don't want to do it," Aaron said. "I've given up. I really have. And I don't want to do it."

"That's nonsense, Aaron, and you know it. We're going to the church, and we're going to earn you some money. Truth is that I could use some myself, that's why I'm going with you. But I'm also doing it as a neighbor."

"There's no such thing as neighbors anymore. We all just live around each other these days, no one lives next to anyone."

"Whatever it is you're doing right now, you need to stop. You're one of the nicest people I know. It's just nonsense, saying that there's no such thing as neighbors. I'm your neighbor."

"Saying a word over and over again doesn't make it real."

"I will beat the shit out of you if you don't stop."

"Fine."

The elevator finally let them out, and they walked along the dark streets of New York City, in the general direction of the church that was a few miles away. The winter sun had set on the day several hours before, but it wasn't cold. Aaron had his fists deep in his pockets and was looking up the towering black façade of every building they passed, silently.

Eventually Aaron spoke. "Don't you think it's amazing that every one of these buildings is full of people like us, just trying to make it? Succeeding and failing, more or less. Just depends on what door you open—this door, things are going great; that door, things couldn't be worse. There's half a billion people in this city alone."

"I told you to stop."

"I'm not arguing. I'm going with you. I'm walking right along, aren't I? I'm just saying. It's all statistics, with a number that large. Pure statistics. Thirty percent of the people in the world have blue as their favorite color. And the average person sleeps six and a half hours a day. And the preferred meal of forty-six percent of the world is chicken and potatoes. Now to the individual person, those numbers don't mean a damn thing. 'My favorite color is purple,' you say. 'And I like beef.' But if you have half a billion people, you look at statistics. You don't care about the individual. And you can build an economy that way. Hell, they have to. When all that matters is efficiency, they decide for the whole world that nine ounces is the perfect serving size for your blue chicken and potato meal, because that's the best number their research can produce. And if your metabolism is just slightly above average, you slowly starve yourself to death, you, the individual, but it doesn't matter because on average everyone is just fine."

"You said you're not arguing, but I don't believe you," Karl said.

"You don't have an opinion on the matter? Am I not stimulating some thought here?"

"No, you're not."

They arrived at the church, a relatively small ten-story building that was made in an imitation-gothic style, with long spires adorning the top. In the elevator, Karl picked a floor, and finally they were in a long, crowded room, hundreds of rows of pews facing a small altar in the distance. The other nine floors were exactly the same in composition, only differing in how far above ground they happened to be. They sat down in the first area they found large enough to fit them both.

It was loud. Everyone around them was talking to themselves, some sitting, some kneeling on the floor, some standing in the aisles. They were all ages, and from all levels of financial wellbeing, although most were obviously impoverished. The person immediately to the right of Aaron was a fifteen-year-old boy, praying fervently with his eyes squeezed shut, childishly.

"I can't promise anything," Aaron said.

"This is as easy as it gets," Karl replied. "You just sit here, and pray. Say nice things about people. Wish people good luck. You don't even have to mean it. Just say it. Talk. You can talk, right? You were doing it well enough on the way here. The money's not great, but it's money."

Aaron turned toward the altar, and for a moment even considered things he might have said aloud that would constitute a prayer, but practically before he had gotten anywhere at all his mind rejected the premise. He realized that he hated the church most of all. Karl had said it himself—he didn't even have to mean it, he just had to say it. The fact that Karl could casually say such a faithless truth while standing in the middle of the church without anyone caring was a testament to how meaningless it was.

Karl had already begun saying his own prayers, so didn't pay attention to the content of Aaron's words when he began to speak—from Karl's perspective, Aaron looked like he was complying. But instead of praying, Aaron said, "Hello, God.

Karma. I'm sitting here in this fine establishment of yours, and I must say I'm disappointed. I don't know what kind of business you're running, but I can't comprehend how it is you still have customers that believe in your product. I've only hinted at it before, but I'll say it directly now, since it seems like the appropriate time and place. I denounce you. I am no longer in your service. I'm retiring. Every word there is for quitting, it applies to me.

"I'll give you a reason or two as well, since I don't want you to think that I haven't put any thought into it. There is no way I can think of that you can take my words, my actions, even my emotions, if you knew them, and assign them a moral value. What does the movement of my arms have to do with how good I am? What do the words I say have to do with how good I am? And the way I feel? I don't feel like the gap between the two can be bridged, between the visible side of things and the moral. It makes sense to me that a perfectly good man could be forced into doing and saying and feeling a lot of horrible things. There's something there that's harder to see, that makes it harder to judge. And, no offense intended, especially by a machine.

"I will grant that you were originally programmed by humans, and so in effect it is still humans judging humans, as it always has been, and perhaps that's as good as it gets. But the human element of that judgment is surprisingly absent now. Forgotten. Now it is you, Karma, that sees the action, tries to understand the context, and then applies the rule. It's the agency of the judgment, the fact that in a real sense it's you making the decisions, that bothers me. It's hard to say clearly, but I feel it strongly.

"I'm tired of these people only doing the right thing because they get paid by you. I want to decide what is right on my own for once. And I don't want a single reward for getting it right. I want my agency back, and it will never happen under your dictatorship, so I'm getting out of here. Goodbye." And he stood up.

Karl, sitting beside him, turned to him when he saw that he was leaving. "Where are you going?" he asked.

"To the bathroom."

Out on the street, Aaron decided that a bar was the best place for him. Nearly without an exception, all of the public bars were also Privacy Rooms, and that was exactly what he needed at that moment. He needed to be off the map, and to stop thinking about things so much. It was tearing him apart, destroying him mentally.

"Drunken Monkey it is," he said to the first bar that he came across. "It was simply meant to be, you and I meeting here. It's fate. Something the machines wouldn't understand." And he went inside.

There was the perfect amount of sad, lonely people for his taste. He made sure to sit at least two places away from the nearest person as he took a seat at the bar. He ordered a beer and looked around him.

Some people were playing billiards at a table not too far away. Neither of them were very good, which they seemed to find hilarious and acceptable. On one of the televisions was some talk show where some nicely dressed gentleman was being interviewed by some other nicely dressed gentleman. The volume was loud enough that he could hear what they were talking about over the din of the bar. He realized quickly that the man being interviewed was Charles Darcy, the modern hero he had been reading about a while before. He listened as he drank a few beers.

When the interview was over, Aaron said to himself, "What an idiot, this Charles. Bless his too-full, little heart. Could he honestly feel the way he says he feels? I don't believe it. He's just faking it like absolutely everyone else, all those people in that damn church. He's just faking it a lot better. So he's an even bigger idiot."

He turned to the bartender. "One more please."

The bartender shook his head.

"No… no what?" Aaron asked, confused.

"I'm cutting you off."

"Cutting me off? I'm not even drunk. I'll admit I was hoping to get there, but this is a bar after all, it's not like I came to the wrong place."

"I'm not cutting you off because you're drunk."

"Then what is it?"

The bartender pointed to Aaron's Karma Card, which was lying on the counter so that he could keep track of the money he was drinking away. "The Tax is coming up here soon. You can't afford this."

Aaron was unbelievably perturbed. "First the machines are judging me, and now bartenders? Bartenders! First my wife is spying on me, and now bartenders? What is this world? It's not the one I signed up for." He snatched his Card up off the table. "I'm going to a place where my patronage is appreciated."

"I would strongly recommend against that," the bartender responded. When Aaron had gone, the bartender looked at his own Karma Card. He had earned one hundred dollars, for reminding a wayward man about the Tax. It was a good time of year for his business.

7

WILL WAS AT one of the Rehabilitation clinics, receiving training in preparation for the few weeks after the Tax. Once again, Lieutenant Caplan was the one showing the group of new officers around, pointing out various things and explaining them tersely. Some of the people that made up the group had been officers for considerably longer than Will, but due to timing knew as little about the Rehabilitation clinics as he did.

"This is the main entrance, if you couldn't tell by the large gates. You're going to stand right here with the person you arrested, and wait for the screen of your Karma Card to change. When it does, you'll hit accept. They'll send two people out and escort you in. If you can see those people up there, up in those towers, those are some of the guards. All guards here have an extended range of twenty feet on their Evaporation Pens, so they can hit you even from up there." Caplan hit a few buttons on his own Karma Card, and soon a group of uniformed men came out to greet them.

"Okay, we're going in."

All around them were men armed with thick vests and absurdly little Evaporation Pens. They all wore expressions of advanced disinterest. Will couldn't quite tell why, but he knew already that he didn't like it there. They were about twenty minutes outside of the city limits, in a place he had never heard of before.

"It isn't entirely necessary for you to know why the people you arrest are arrested, but I'm going to tell you anyway, for clarity's sake. As you know, the Tax is based on age, gender, and economic status, but it's going to be roughly two thousand dollars no matter who you are. And if you don't pay it in time, this is where you end up. There is no forgiveness for lateness and no exceptions to the rule, so don't be calling your superiors saying that the person you arrested says they are a special case and didn't have to pay at the same time, or anything like that. They will be lying to you, and a lot of them do at that point.

"Here are some things you perhaps didn't know, or didn't think of. Some of you might think that the way we treat people in here is harsh, but just remember that the Tax was established to make sure everyone's doing their fair share of work throughout the year. We don't want any people freeloading on the system. The people in Rehabilitation, if they prove themselves to be valuable citizens to society at any point during their detainment here, are free to go. But only if they show promise. The people that don't show a will to reform their ways will be here the rest of their life. You'll see some old people in here—some of them are new additions, some of them have been here longer than any of you have been alive. Just keep that in mind. I've always considered this a good time to remind you that your own Tax rate has gone up a little bit, but your new Good Work rate should more than compensate for that. Just don't be surprised when you see the bill."

They were passing by prison cells, one after the other, all filled with emaciated people, all wearing orange. There were women and men alike, and Will was glad that he didn't see many children as they went by. "We're on our way to the Rehabilitation room, just so you can see what that's like. We want to give you a good idea of what it is we're doing here. Now it used to be, even up until recently, that this place had its fair share of violent criminals too. But ever since violence was reclassified as a felony, all the violent people are just Evaporated. Everyone here either couldn't afford their Tax, or was tampering with their Privacy Room, or that kind of thing. Basically, people that have morally lost their way. But we believe that we can show them the right way again."

The long hallway of prison cells opened up into a large, open room, full of prisoners in orange uniform. He didn't understand what most of them were doing. Some were in large circles, talking, but others seemed to be acting out scenes, complete with props.

"Only about a tenth of the detainees fit in here at a time. They're opening up some more facilities here soon, so the crowding should be a little less by the time you're here again. As you can see, they're all acting out Good Works, kind of like practice, only for them it's learning. They're learning how to open doors for each other over there by that group of doors, they're learning how to pick dropped items for each other over there, and how to compliment each other over there. It's all really good practice, and they even get paid a small rate for it. If, during some Tax, they can ever afford to pay what they owe, they're let out. But the food costs them too, and their entertainment, so it really takes a strong aptitude for goodness to get out of here. But that's exactly what we're trying to do, so it works out great. And we have a reasonably good success rate."

The gaze of one of the prisoners caught Will's own as the

group made their way across the room, and he stopped immediately. It was the strongest resentment he'd ever seen expressed towards him, from a young girl that was picking up a shoe for an old man that had intentionally dropped it for her to pick up. It was entirely in her eyes, the mouth gave away nothing, and she wasn't even furrowing her eyebrows. It was hardly perceptible at all, and yet Will knew beyond doubt that it was there. He wanted to talk to her. She was only ten feet away from him.

The group had already moved on, and it was just him and the surrounding prisoners. "Why?" he asked, meeting her intense, accusatory gaze as best as he could. "Why?" he asked again, when she didn't respond. He couldn't understand her resentment. Perhaps she was mad because he was free and she wasn't, and the Rehabilitation clinic did look like a horrendous place. But she only had herself to blame, and she should have known that.

Will had never had difficulty doing the right thing, so he couldn't understand her failure to do the same, the failure that had led her to Rehabilitation. And then he realized that the failure to understand and do what was right was probably also the failure to understand justice when she saw it, so her resentment was really just a deep misunderstanding, embedded in her character. He wanted to help her, just that one person, but already he was being called.

"Officer Spector, focus. Please stay with the group. We're on a time schedule here," Lieutenant Caplan yelled, from across the room. With effort, Will broke the eye contact established between him and the girl. He tried to push it out of his mind as he rejoined the group.

Later that day, back at the police station, Will was overhearing a conversation between his mentor, Eric, and another officer. Eric was saying, "That Charles Darcy guy, he just keeps getting more and more popular. It's kind of disgusting really. Did you know I was the one that they had offer him a Government position? I talked to the bastard. He was sitting in the City Park, reading some book. Everyone's making it sound like the guy's a hero, but I sensed something really off about him when I talked to him back then. I hope he makes a huge mistake here soon, or just disappears, so I don't have to hear any more about him."

Will was fairly shocked. He had read all there was to read about Charles, and had admired his dedication to society. He couldn't help but to intrude on the conversation of the two officers. "What do you mean by that?"

Eric looked at Will for a second before answering. "I mean exactly what I said. The guy's just suspicious. It was the way he talked. And he was hanging out in the City Park. I don't trust anybody that makes a habit of being in that place. It's not like it's very pretty, or like there's really that much 'nature' in it, and that's the only reason I could see anybody being there, other than the fact that it's the largest Privacy Room in the whole city."

"Well, have you looked into it?" Will persisted.

"I haven't had the time, since I got assigned to look after you. And like I was saying, if he's really up to something then he'll be found out sooner or later, whether I'm watching or not. Karma's unbelievably good at spotting those kinds of things." With that the conversation was over, Eric had gone back to talking about something else entirely with the other officer, leaving Will to think.

He'd had a lot of abrupt surprises, ever since becoming an officer, and that conversation was one of the larger ones for him. In his former life as an ordinary citizen, he never would have questioned even once the heroism of a man like Charles. But once he began to question it, he didn't stop. He sifted through everything he had read about the man, and tried to figure out what was so patently false about any of it.

"He seems sincere," Will thought to himself, thinking of the interview he had watched on television. And he had always felt he had a deep perception of those kinds of things. "When did I get deceived?"

That night, he went home and took his Karma Map out of his large bag of equipment. He wanted to see for himself what was suspicious about Charles Darcy, wherever he was. It had occurred to him earlier that he could do exactly that, with his Karma Map.

He hadn't quite figured out all of the buttons yet, but he tried just speaking Charles' name into the Map several times, to see if it could figure out what he wanted on its own. It did, it took him to a restaurant, where he was sitting across a table from some other middle-aged man, in his hand a glass of wine. He kept glancing up at the people around him, who were all discreetly staring, which was an odd sensation for Will, who felt like it was him they were staring at and had never experienced such a strange sensation.

The man across the table was speaking about a delivery of uniforms, which struck Will as odd. What did a private citizen need a bunch of uniforms for? They only mentioned it briefly, then Charles was talking about a common friend of the two, who Charles seemed to be expressing some concern for.

"I'm worried about Peril. It must be hard for him, doing what he does. But he's the only man I trust, really. If the circumstances were any different, I would tell him that he had done enough, thank him, and have someone else do it. But there is no one else. And he knows how to make a Good Work out of any situation, that's a strong quality in a man."

Will didn't know what was meant about the first part, but he strongly agreed with the last statement, since it resonated deeply with his own values as a citizen. Will said to himself, "He doesn't know that anyone's listening, and that's still the kind of thing he says. A man like that couldn't be suspect."

But he wasn't satisfied, he kept watching. For hours and hours he watched, late into the night. Whenever Charles went to a bathroom, the screen became blank for a while, the only thing remaining on the screen being the Karma logo at the top right, but when he emerged again, Will was right there with him.

Charles went home. One thing Will had always found somewhat at odds with the man's character was the absurdly large house he lived in, which was decorated lavishly with tapestries, vases, and even sculptures. He had seen pictures before of the man's house. The images of Charles' own eyes had been given by Karma's permission to the newspaper, which had published them in an article about how the man lived. It all seemed extremely excessive for a single man, in a world like the one they lived in.

He also noticed, when Charles entered the only bathroom

in the house, that there wasn't a mirror in front of the sink, which he saw momentarily before the screen went to black. "It must be modesty," Will thought to himself. "The man doesn't have a single mirror in his house, as important as his image must be to someone of his popularity. That's a strong character."

It was three in the morning, but Charles was on a subway back into the city, doing a Good Work even as Will watched, and he had never slept at all. Will found it odd that Charles no longer said a single word, everything he did was noiseless. Earlier, Charles had always seemed to be talking, to everyone he met. Perhaps his spirit quieted at night. In the city, he got up from his seat and waited at the door to be let out into the station. Something caught Will's attention, and frantically he tried to pause the scene. He hit some other button on accident, one that zoomed out and took a broad view of the station, where he could see everything from above, and the few people trickling out of the subway before it left for the next station.

"Go back, damn it," Will said to the Map. "Go back right now." He tried tapping again on the dot that represented Charles' perspective. Again he was seeing things from his eyes, as he took the staircase up into the city. "Rewind, rewind." A control panel popped up in the bottom part of the screen. He pressed the rewind button, and then the pause button when he was standing at the door of the subway again, the nearly empty station visible on the other side of the glass.

It was indistinct, but Will felt it with a dead certainty. A reflection could barely be made out from the glass of the subway. It wasn't Charles. It was a man that looked a lot like Charles, the same stature, the same haircut, the same eyes and the same distant smile. But it was a different person. He didn't even know how he knew. He spent a few minutes, staring at the frozen screen, trying to put a finger on what was different about the slightly distorted reflection from all of the pictures he'd seen before. He ended up giving up. But he was confident regardless.

It was nearly four in the morning, but he called Eric. A rough, sleepy voice answered the call. "What is it, Will?" he said on the other end.

"I found something. I don't know what it is, though. I was watching Charles. I believe you now, he's up to something."

The voice became more awake, more alert. "What did you find?"

"Is it possible for two people to be one person? It doesn't seem possible to me, but I'm looking at this picture and it's the only conclusion I can come to."

"What are you talking about?"

"I'm looking at the reflection of whoever it is that's using Charles' Karma Chip, and it's not him. Now I'm asking, is that possible?"

"No, it isn't."

"Why not?" Will argued.

"Karma would have noticed. And you can't use the same Chip. They're too complicated for any citizen to understand, much less build and manipulate."

"What if Karma wasn't looking, because it didn't expect it either? I don't think it's impossible, is all I'm saying."

"Well, you show me whatever it is you're looking at when we're at work today, and I'll tell you what I think."

"Okay."

"Goodnight, rookie. Get some sleep. If you're really up this late, looking into that kind of thing, you're trying too hard."

8

JACKSON, A LONGTIME member of Charles' Order, sat at a bench in the City Park, waiting for a man to sit down next to him. Even though the sky was grey as always, it was agreed that the man would be wearing sunglasses, so that Jackson could identify him. He had almost given up waiting when the man appeared from around a copse of withered trees, following one of the main paths that honeycombed the Park. Without acknowledging Jackson in the slightest, he sat down next to him.

Jackson waited a minute or two before asking, "Damon? Is that your name?"

"Yes, yes it is," the man answered, nervously.

"And you're sure that you want to do this? You've weighed your options?"

"I can't afford the Tax, I don't have any other options. I'm joining. Now can you tell me what's going on? I still don't know what it is I'm doing, really. No one has told me."

"It's still too early for that," Jackson said. "But if you're sure that you're committing, the answer to that question isn't too far off. I'll just need your help with a few things first."

"With what?"

"Just say that you will help."

"I will."

"Okay. Stand up. You're going to go straight to a medical supply store. You're going to buy some gauze, painkillers, and some anesthetics. Like you cut your leg pretty bad or something, those kinds of things. Buy the good stuff for the anesthetic, you'll be glad you did. You're going to steal a scalpel. Now I know that's illegal, and that you'd get caught eventually, but don't worry about it. Do it. It's very important that you do. And then you're going to go to a hardware store, and buy a saw. Don't ask why. And then you're going to go straight to your apartment, and then to your bathroom. Leave the door to your apartment ajar, but don't look back at it while you're doing it. Bring all the stuff into the bathroom with you, don't just leave it on your counter or the whole thing is going to be ruined, got it? And when you're in your bathroom, don't leave, no matter what happens. I will be there shortly, and then I'll tell you the rest. Got it?"

The man simply nodded.

"Then go. And do it quickly. And nothing suspicious, besides what can't be avoided." When the man had hurried off, Jackson stood up himself and walked farther along the path, to another bench where two men were already sitting. "He's on his way. Do you have the body already?"

One of the men responded, "It's in a dumpster outside his place. He's good, then?"

"I said he was on his way, didn't I? Now let's go."

The three men had to walk all the way to the man's apartment, since they couldn't use the subway. It was about five miles. When they had gotten there, they went behind the building, into a secluded alleyway with a large dumpster up against the building. They sat in the corner it formed with the wall. Jackson took a Karma Map out of the backpack he carried with him. He turned it on, and pressed a few buttons, until finally he was seeing the world from the eyes of the man he had just sent off, Damon. He was on a subway, the bag of supplies in his hand.

"He's almost here. I'd say we have about five minutes." He pressed a few more buttons, and was looking at a map of the apartment complex, specifically at the elevators and hallways. He watched for several minutes. "There are quite a few people going around. I'd say that your safest bet is the elevator you'll find if you go right, and then all of the way to the back of the building. There doesn't seem to be as many people back there. You do have the body here?"

One of the other men stood up, opened the lid to the dumpster, and looked down into it. "Yeah, he's still here."

"Get him out," Jackson said. They jumped in, and heaved a large bag up and out of the dumpster, setting it carefully on the ground next to Jackson. Jackson opened the bag, and inspected the corpse carefully. "Good, very good."

He then looked quickly inside two backpacks that had been inside the bag with the body. "This one's his," he said, as he handed one of them over to one of the men. The other backpack he traded with his own. "Okay, our guy's already in the elevator up to his place. Go ahead."

The two men stood the dead body up, put the backpack on its shoulders, put a hat on it, and then put its arms around their shoulders. "Does it look good?" one of them asked.

"Beautiful, just beautiful. Take him up. I'll be right behind." With that they started walking around to the front of the building, body in tow. Jackson put the empty bag back into the dumpster, put the other backpack on, and then went himself.

At the main entrance, a man was opening the door for people going in. When he saw three men, two carrying the third between them, he was quick to open the door for them. "Doesn't look good for that one," he said, indicating the dead body.

"Drunk off his ass," one of them said. "We're helping him get back to his place."

"Bless your hearts," the man that was holding the door said. "Let me get this for you, it's the least I could do."

"Thank you very much."

They took the body as quickly as they could to the elevator in the back, smiling and explaining their situation with a few words to everyone they passed. They were lucky to catch an empty elevator up to Damon's floor, and no one got on as the elevator ascended. When they had finally arrived at the right floor, they saw Jackson on the far side of the hall of doors, gesturing them over. The door he was standing in front of was slightly ajar, which they pushed open. They went straight for the bathroom.

"Hello Damon," he said, when he opened the bathroom door. "Good to see you here. Bring him in," he said to the men that were standing out in the kitchen. "And you, Damon, stand in your shower. We need the space."

The two men dragged the dead body into the bathroom, and set it on the toilet seat. Jackson took the backpack off of it, opened it up, and pulled out a compact machine. He then opened his own backpack, pulled out a similar machine, and joined the two together by securing a few latches.

"We don't have much time," Jackson said to Damon, who

was standing with a confused look in his shower. "Where's the anesthetic?"

"In that brown bag on the sink," Damon said.

"Now, you're not going to like the sound of this, Damon, but I'm going to have to remove your ear. I'm not going to lie to you, it's going to hurt like hell, even with this anesthetic. And you won't recover for a week or two. But I've done like fifty of these and I've never killed a dude, alright?" The man just nodded dumbly. Jackson mounted the machine on the wall above the shower with suction cups. The two other men had already begun to partially cut a portion of the dead man's skull off, after which they turned him upside down and drained him on the floor.

"You're making a mess," Damon complained.

"Shut up and hold still," Jackson said, a syringe in his hand.

Three hours later, while they were walking north, Jackson had the group of men stop for a second, while he showed an extremely drowsy Damon his Karma Map. "Watch this. Damon, hey Damon. Watch this."

The man slowly opened his eyes, and looked at the screen Jackson was holding in front of him. "Hey," he said slowly. "That's my bathroom." On the small, circular screen could be seen the dead body from before, slumped over and bloody, sitting on the toilet and head resting against the sink. The details of the face were obscured by blood.

A saw was lying on the ground, a scalpel in the sink, and an overturned bottle of pills was scattered everywhere. A hand was extended from the perspective of the screen, as if it was the hand of whoever was looking into the bathroom. In their hand was a small pen. Suddenly a bright light emitted from it, and the body was gone.

"What? What just happened?" Damon asked, confused.

"You're Dead now, remember that. You're one of the Dead."

Eight miles away, standing in the air of an Evaporated man, Marcus looked around quickly to make sure that nothing suspicious had been left behind. There weren't any backpacks, or suction cups, or anything else that would catch the eye of a supercomputer. He was satisfied.

For the first time in quite a while, Charles was visiting his Monastery. He told Vincent to gather everyone to the temple, since it was a Sunday and he wanted to give a sermon. Half of the people were already there, meditating. The other half were on the farm, and had to be brought in. When they had all finally crowded into the small, wooden edifice, he began without delay.

"In the very near future, our Order will be called upon to prove its worth. Some of you will lose your life, and I am sorry. The cost is high, but remember what we're here for. In five short years, the colonization of Mars will begin. We have much less time than that. Right now, Mars is at its most beautiful. Its waters and skies are blue, its trees are green, there are actually wild animals on it, engineered from DNA fragments of extinct species that used to walk this Earth.

"In the next couple months, they will start building obscene buildings. A Sky Kite to blot out the sky, large skyscrapers to replace the trees, one by one. They will tell you that this Sky Kite is more transparent than the last, but I tell you from the perspective of science that it can't be entirely transparent, or it wouldn't do the job that it is there for, which is to absorb sun, and therefore to block the sun, and make energy from it. They will tell you the buildings will be more beautiful this time, designed by the best architects in the field, but they will always be oblong, metal things that require more energy than they create, or in other words are entirely unnatural. They will tell you the animals will be at home there, but I'm telling you now that they'll die again like they died before, if a large change isn't made moving forward.

"I brought you all here, to the Monastery, to try to prove one thing to you. That if you put a lot of your own energy into it, your life is sustainable. You don't need the factories to produce a living for you, you can plant seeds and raise animals and do it yourself. I feel like it's a lesson often forgotten. Everyone feels that it's best that everything remotely unpleasant is done for them, leaving them to do whatever they want, which for whatever historical reason has evolved into Good Works. In my opinion, this evolution was a misstep. We evolved wrong. I want to turn back the biological clock, and give us another chance. There is no reason that a Good Work has to be defined as directly helping your fellow brother. You can help your fellow brother just as well by doing your Good Works to the Earth itself, by removing the Solar Kites and the factories and using your own energy, by being your own factory.

"These views would be considered heretical by Karma, or at the very least they would never be rewarded. Which is the same as being heretical, because in this society you have to constantly be 'rewarded' just to survive. Nor is the oversight of Karma natural. Somehow a machine, a supercomputer, was placed above us as the ultimate authority. It constantly invades our privacy—these 'Privacy Rooms' are not a consolation for the damage that is done the rest of the time. Everywhere you go, you are being watched, almost all the way to your very thoughts. This is why we declared Karma as our enemy, this machine, and declared the true karma as our savior in its place, the harmony and oneness with the Earth and the universe around it. So I took the Chip out of your head, at least half of the time. Moving forward, moving onto Mars, I promise to take it out of your head all the time, if I am able. But I'm going to need your help.

"As I said, it's the next few months that are extremely important. We need to make the change before they start building a new, stronger Karma on Mars. Because that's exactly what they'll do. When they built this Karma, they didn't realize how central it would be to the world. So even though it is protected very well, up on the ninety-third floor of the Karma Tower, it isn't invincible. On Mars, they will plan it better. They will put it underground, they will put it everywhere, into the earth itself, where it will never be possible to eradicate it entirely. It will be invincible. For the good of mankind, we will prevent that eventuality by destroying Karma now.

"I hope this doesn't come as a complete surprise to anyone. Out of necessity, I haven't shared many of the details with you, until this point. If anyone else knew what we were doing, we would have all been dead long ago. So I kept it a secret, as hard as that is to do these days. We, as an Order, have been building an ideology for the past two years, but we've also been building a lot of weapons. In the other half of this building, on the other side of the wall behind me, we have our own monitoring system, as you know. We also have our own Evaporation Pens, our own Grappling Chains, and our own explosives, that we made ourselves. It is not a coincidence that I made the two separate functions part of the same building, the temple and the armory. I believe that they are two facets of the same object.

"Over the next few days, instead of meditating, you will be trained on how to use these weapons. Of course, half of you will still be maintaining the farm, or our system will collapse. We'll take turns, like we always have.

"Now I want a show of hands. How many of you are opposed to this plan? And feel free to be honest and express your true feelings on the matter. That is, after all, what we are here for, to protect human dignity and the right to dissent. If you do object, I won't let you go back into the city, and give us away, but I will let you stay here permanently, which shouldn't be objectionable, because it's what some of you have been doing for years now. Please, let me see the hands of those that don't want to proceed with us."

Not a single person raised their hand. It was what he had hoped for, it definitely made things less complicated if everyone went along with him. He had spent the last few years developing their loyalty for that purpose alone.

"That's very good, that's what I wanted to see. I will conclude today's sermon with that display of solidarity, since I feel that it embodies our mission so well. Half of you will now return to the farm, and the other half will commence training immediately. Thank you," he said, and he stepped down from the pulpit.

9

ERIC HAD TAKEN Will to a Privacy Room inside of the police station, where they were looking at Will's Karma Map.

"I don't see what you're seeing, Will, but like I told you before I think the guy's suspicious, so I can almost believe you. Even though it's unbelievable."

"So what do we do about it?" Will asked, excited.

"If you're really up for this, I'll get a small group of people—I'm thinking Steve, John, and Marcus. Don't tell anyone else. If we can expose this man, and take him out all on our own, we'll be heroes. I know how much you've always wanted to be a hero, I've been watching you for this past month. If you're right, this will be that time. But until we bring him down, you can't tell anyone. Don't go around telling everyone you know that Charles Darcy is somehow breaking the system. I'll tell you why.

"It has happened before, that people have successfully gotten the Karma Chip out of their head. That's not the kind of thing they teach you in school, even in training here, because I don't think they want you to know. I don't think I'm even supposed to know. You've already seen the kind of desperate people that try to cut their own Chip out. Most of them don't even think it was possible, even as they do it. It's just desperation that tells them they should. Some of them have said that same thing to me, right before I Evaporated them. 'It isn't possible. I knew I was going to die instead.' There would be a lot more people out there trying to get their Chip out, if they knew it was possible to get it out and keep living. I could guarantee you that. And that's why they don't want people to know, I think. They go around telling you that you need it to live, they say it's as important to the functioning of your brain as your spinal cord, in schools and in the newspapers, so people don't mess with it.

"What I'm trying to say is, if you go around telling people Charles got his Chip out of his head, I think that Karma might start investigating you as well, as weird as that sounds, and you don't want that. Because you doubted for a second what they taught you in school, about the Card being necessary for life. So it's our secret. I'm telling you this because I trust you, okay man? And we're going to go do this, so I need you to be on the same page, alright?"

"Alright."

"We're going to get our little group together, and we're just going to go out there, to where this Charles guy lives. We're not going to even give a reason. And if we find some Privacy Room he's be tampering with, or some other electronics, that will be good enough, we'll have him. Okay?"

"Okay."

"I'll talk to the other guys, and then we'll go. Right away, so get ready."

The five of them were on a subway headed to Champlain, New York. Will was sitting next to Marcus, and the usually laconic man was talking to him for the first time in the month that Will had been working with him. "What is it we're doing here? Eric didn't tell me anything."

The rest of the officers were a few seats down, outside of earshot. Will said, "We're going to go check out Charles Darcy. You've heard of the guy, right? He's pretty famous now. That guy that got rich doing Good Works."

"And why are we doing that?"

He didn't know how much he should say. He wasn't in a Privacy Room, for one thing, and Eric had apparently not deemed it important to tell the others the situation. But Will didn't have much of a capacity for lying, or evading questions, so he tried to answer without directly disobeying Eric's advice.

"I just… we just thought he was kind of suspicious. Eric said he'd thought he was suspicious ever since he talked to him in the City Park. You went with him, didn't you? Or was it someone else?"

"It was me," Marcus said.

"And you didn't think there was anything suspicious about him?"

Just then they stopped at another station, and a large group of elderly people got onto the subway. Most were able to find a seat, but an elderly man was left standing in the middle of the aisle, looking around him futilely. Will stood up. "You can sit here, sir. I'll just stand."

"No, that's alright, young man," he said, although without much conviction in his voice, as he stared at the empty seat.

"I'm insisting," Will said, and distanced himself from the seat more.

"Alright, alright. Thank you."

Will then stood in front of Marcus as the subway started

up again, and was still waiting expectantly for an answer. "You were saying?" Will prompted.

"Oh, suspicious? Not terribly, no. Some people just like to go to the Park, even if it is ugly. That's probably what Eric told you he thought was weird about him, right? That he liked to hang out in the Park? Eric just can't understand that some people like the little relics of nature that we still have left."

"That is what he said, but that's not why I'm convinced."

"Then why are you convinced?"

"It's hard to say," he said, hesitantly.

"Charles is a guy that's been doing Good Works every second of his waking life, and he doesn't sleep. I would have figured that would be right up your alley. You seem like a pretty diligent guy. Is it jealousy?"

"Jealousy? No. It's something else. I mean, I guess we'll just see when we get there. We'll either find something, or we won't."

"Very true," Marcus said. "I'm very interested to see which it will be."

They stood at the front door of Charles' mansion, and Eric had just rung. They waited, somewhat tensely, for a response. After two minutes, Eric said to the others, "He's in there. I can see him on my Karma Map. We rang the doorbell, and he went to the bathroom. Make any sense to you guys? If he takes any longer, I say we just break in."

Only a second after Eric had finished speaking, the door opened and Charles was standing behind it, fairly worn looking but still handsome. "Can I help you?" he asked, a little out of breath.

"We're here to inspect the place," Eric said with authority. "And I'll be asking you a few questions, if you'll show me around."

"Naturally. Please, do come in. And I know it's a quaint tradition, but if you could leave your shoes by the door, I would appreciate it," he said as he backed up, and opened the door wider to let them in. Everyone but Eric took their shoes off. Will was embarrassed by his metallic feet, which looked so conspicuous among the rest. While they were all still at the entrance, Eric whispered into Will's ear, "Check the bathroom. Thoroughly. There's a reason he went in there first. Ask him where it is."

"Mr. Darcy," Will started, after Eric had backed away from him. "If you could point me in the direction of the bathroom, please?"

"It's right down that hall, to your left. You won't be able to miss it."

"And take me to the master bedroom, or wherever it is you sleep," Eric said, when Will had finished.

"Oh, you're the man from before, aren't you? That I met in the City Park. I just recognized you. Pleasure to see you again. If you're offering a position again, now isn't the best time."

"That's not why we're here. The master bedroom."

"My mistake. Right this way."

While they walked down the halls and up the stairs, past all of the tapestries and portraits hanging on the walls, Eric had his Karma Map out, and was inspecting it carefully. Finally Charles stopped in front of a door, and opened it for them.

"Here you have it. Be my guest."

"This isn't your bedroom," Eric said, before even looking into it.

"What on earth does that mean?" Charles asked, genuinely confused.

"It's not a Privacy Room."

"Do I have to sleep in it to convince you? Or what? You can stay around for that if you want to, and I'll try. But I don't sleep, and I don't have much need for a bedroom, so I didn't even bother having one installed. The only Privacy Room is the bathroom downstairs that your young friend is using."

"And where does a rich man like you take the ladies when they come over, then?" Eric continued.

"If you mean what I think you mean, I'm celibate, and there's none of that."

"Celibate? Celibate?"

"Am I not answering your questions properly? I'm sorry, but once again I've been sort of caught off guard by your rudeness, and am having a hard time adjusting."

"Can you take us to the kitchen?"

"Right this way."

Downstairs, Will was working his way methodically through the bathroom. There was still no mirror above the sink, just like he'd seen it on his Map. He thought he would start there, since it was the most conspicuous. He felt around all of the edges, and rapped his fist against the walls to see if they sounded hollow. He turned all of the knobs on and off on the sink and in the shower, and the light switches on and off. He accidentally broke one of the handles off of the sink, a problem he'd been having ever since he had started taking the steroids prescribed to him by the police. The new strength in his hands, and in his body, seemed excessive. He laid the broken handle on the counter. Then he flushed the toilet and took the porcelain top off of it.

"How ancient is this toilet?" he asked himself. He had never seen anything like it. And the floor was tile, which he had never seen in a bathroom before either. He picked up the rug off the ground, to see what was under it.

The Privacy Room, the small triangles in the corner, seemed normal to him as well. When he thought he had tried everything, he left and rejoined the group, which was by then in the kitchen.

Eric was still rapidly asking questions. "Did you have the place inspected and certified, when you moved in?"

"Surely you have the paperwork for that yourself. It was one of your very own officers that looked the place over, and installed the Privacy Room in the bathroom for me. So I don't know why you're asking."

"If you say so," Eric responded. He then walked up to the large window on the far side of the kitchen, which overlooked an expansive open field, with trees in the distance, the likes of which were unseen in the city.

"How much of that is yours."

"All of it, I think."

"Why haven't you ever gone out there?"

"You keep on saying things that I honestly don't understand. How would you know that I've never gone out there? Does Karma keep track of that kind of thing?"

Eric showed him the screen of his Karma Map. "These are all places that you've been, around this house. And you've never gone out there. Apparently no one has, ever since Karma started keeping track. Now why is that?"

"You can really do that? That's amazing. I've never seen that. I suppose I just haven't felt like going out there. But surely that isn't a crime, like you're making it sound."

"You take a one hour subway all the way into New York City just to sit in your little City Park, for your 'nature,' but you don't ever even go into your own backyard?"

"Well there aren't as many benches in my backyard. Maybe if I ever get that fixed I'll switch to that. And there's so many nice people you meet on the subway."

Eric's patience was tested to its limits with Charles. For a while he was silent. Will took the opportunity to whisper to Eric, "I couldn't find anything. I don't know why, because like you said he had to be doing something."

"I'm going to go look myself," Eric said to Will, at a normal volume. "You ask him a few questions of your own. I'll be back."

While he was walking away, Charles said, indicating Marcus, "You still don't talk much, now do you. I'm starting to wonder what they keep you around for. Is there something you do?"

Marcus didn't answer. Will ignored the question as well. "Is there a reason you don't have any mirrors in the place? I couldn't help but notice."

"That's very perceptive of you. There's nothing a mirror is very good for, if you think about it. I just don't see the use."

"I don't see the use of a lot of the decoration you have around the place, either."

"For a second I thought you might be less aggressive than the other, but there you go. Well, I assure you that all of these pots and pictures are far prettier than me, and I keep them around for that."

"You don't live with anyone else?"

"No, I don't."

"In a house this large."

"I might get it downsized if I don't figure out a way to use some of the rooms."

Before Will could think of another question, his Karma Card began to ring. So did everyone else's around him, with the exception of Charles. Eric returned from the hallway. "Are you getting this too?" he asked, pointing to his Card. "Did you see this?"

They all nodded.

"We have to go. We'll be back, Mr. Darcy. Some other time."

The directions on the Karma Card were far more descriptive than Will had ever seen them be before. He was to get off at stop R2-J, which was right next to a Karma Card manufacturing plant on the outskirts of the city. There were people attacking it, at that very moment. He was only to use his stun gun, so that the attackers could be interrogated. It said that the attackers were well armed. Everyone else's Card said the same thing.

"This is pretty serious, isn't it."

"I've never seen anything like it," John said, one of the other officers in their group.

"Can I leave my bag somewhere? I feel like it's going to get in the way," Will said, looking at the bulky thing he'd been carrying around everywhere with him.

"You can do whatever you want with it, but if you lose anything in it you'll have to buy replacements yourself, and I promise you that you don't want to do that."

"But there's nowhere on the subway, I mean?"

"No, not really."

"Fine," Will said. "I just feel like I'm going to die, and it will be because I'll be too busy carrying this huge bag around while everyone is shooting at me."

"Good luck with that," Eric said.

When the subway pulled up to the subway station, already explosions could be heard from above. "I don't want to go," Steve said. "This is absurd."

"Don't be a pansy," Eric said.

Will took the two sets of handcuffs he had out of his bag, the normal and the high-torsion. He also took his Karma Map, his stun gun, and his Grappling Chain, and put them all in his pockets, except for the stun gun that he kept in his hand. The rest he left in the bag. When the doors of the subway opened, he ran out, and as he passed the benches that filled the station, he threw his bag under one of them. Everyone else followed, slightly less enthusiastic than he was.

Above ground there was fire everywhere, and several officers were lying around on the ground, bleeding from various wounds. He looked around for someone that seemed coherent enough to tell him what was going on.

"Where are they?" he yelled, over another explosion in the background. The man was sitting on the ground, holding his knee and rocking back and forth. He simply pointed to a hole in the wall of a building that was twenty feet away from them, out of which smoke was pouring. "Over there? Thank you!" he yelled, as he was already running off.

As he entered the building through the hole, he was shot in the left shoulder by a bullet. By a gun, a real gun. He didn't think that any existed. The man that had shot him was standing right next to him, and was preparing to shoot him again. With quick reflexes, Will paralyzed him with his stun gun, and watched him crumple to the ground. He could hear noises of movement ahead of him, so he ran on.

Twenty feet ahead of him, another man had turned around and began shooting at Will. The range of Will's stun gun was far less than twenty feet, so he shot the man with his Grappling Chain, directly in the chest, and anchored himself on the ground. The man flew toward him, and, as soon as he was within arm's length, Will punched him in the face and into the ground, where he then shot him with his stun gun.

A group of men had climbed a staircase, and were shooting at him from a platform above. Will shot the corner of the ledge below them with his Grappling Chain, which took him up as soon as it latched on. Right before he reached the end of its length, he pulled as hard as he could on the remaining chain with the arm that wasn't holding the gun, so that it sent him flying high over the platform, where he started trying to stun them from above before he landed. One of them shot him in his hip, he stunned two others, and the third one he had to kick off of the platform, through the railing, to avoid being shot pointblank.

He looked around to his left and right, but couldn't see any more people, so he took out his Karma Map and zoomed in on himself. There was one more man, further down the hallway he was in, that he could see if he scrolled over. He put the Map away and continued onward.

The man was standing in front of a large steel door. Loud machines could be heard on the other side, and the room felt full of their vibrations. The man was placing a large explosive against the wall, and pressing buttons on it. Will shot him in the back with his Grappling Chain, and whipped him into the wall to his side as he flew past, where he made a loud cracking noise.

He walked up to the explosive, to see what it said. It was flashing the number ten over and over again. He wasn't sure, but he thought that he had stopped them from doing whatever it was they were doing.

Then he was shot again, a bullet cutting across the side of his neck. He sidestepped to avoid another shot, which embedded itself into the wall where he had been. He tried jumping behind a short wall to take cover, but ended up going twenty feet higher than he thought he would, and hitting his head on the ceiling. He was extremely disoriented as he fell back down, and landed on his back on the wall he had been trying to jump over. While he was prostrate, he could see the man taking aim at him again.

Right before he pulled the trigger, he was Evaporated. Eric stood in the place where he had been. "Will, what the hell. You ran off ahead."

"Eric, that man didn't have a Chip. I looked at my Map, that man wasn't here." The other man, the one who had been setting the bomb, was still lying unconscious where Will had thrown him.

"Will, shut up!"

"But it's true, Eric, they're out there! I looked at my Map, right before I walked into this room. And they're wearing uniforms. It's Charles. It has to be."

The other men showed up shortly after, Marcus, Steve, and John. They helped Will to his feet, since he could barely support himself. "I tried jumping," he said, "and somehow I jumped to the ceiling. These damn steroids are throwing me off."

"You mean the shoes, right?" Steve asked.

"What do you mean, the shoes?"

"Did Fred give you your stuff, back when you started? That asshole never tells people what the shoes do. Sure, it's funny when you find out while your outside, but I swear to God someone's going to die because of that dude, trying to jump inside a building."

Will's Karma Card began to ring. One of the other guys, John, pulled it out of his pocket for him. Eric's was ringing as well. The message was the same—it said to go directly to the Karma Tower.

"Damn it, Will. I told you," Eric said.

John read through the rest of the message. "They're sending in a Helicar for you."

10

THE OFFICERS HAD just left Charles' mansion. When he was sure that they were gone, he went straight back to the bathroom. He said to his sink, "Send Brother Peril back in. They're gone."

While he was waiting, he shaved his head, put in contacts that changed the color of his eyes, and changed into some ragged, oversized clothes that he had in a closet next to the bathroom. Then Peril arrived, looking a lot like Charles had only moments before.

"Interesting look you have there, Brother Charles," Peril said, after knocking and waiting to be let in to the bathroom.

"It's time, Brother Peril. For everything we planned. It's all happening."

"Is it really?"

"It is. I need you to go to the Park, and put on the leather gloves, so that the ghosts know they should meet you there. I'll be there right behind you, I just need to go talk to Brother Vincent."

The ghosts were all the people that Charles had in the city without Karma Chips, recruiting new members and doing all the things that people being watched by Karma could never get away with. Jackson's group was one of the many teams he had operating. The main difficulty with having ghosts was that they were nearly impossible to communicate with, so he had to develop strange systems that only ever worked half of the time.

"I'm wearing the gloves? Why am *I* doing it? And what do I tell them when they show up?"

"We don't have that much time, they're already suspicious. The Karma Chip factory will only keep them preoccupied for so long. I told you I'd be there right behind you, I'll talk to them."

"Is there anything special I have to do with the gloves?"

"Just look at them a lot."

"Alright."

"And Brother Peril," Charles said, becoming really serious and quiet.

"Yes?"

"Be really careful. Now more than ever. But make it to the City Park."

In the back of the temple building, Emerson was sitting in a rolling chair, watching the many screens that showed their people in the city. Behind him, a few men were busy soldering away on electrical devices. Charles burst into the building. "Brother Emerson. Where is Brother Vincent?"

"It's not his shift," he responded.

"I don't really care right now."

"He should be in the temple, meditating."

"Thank you."

"And Brother Charles, while I have you, they're bringing in another recruit. What should we do with him?"

"Who's bringing him in?"

"Jackson's group. He just left a message at checkpoint delta, so he should be here within a few hours."

Charles tripped momentarily over the triviality of dealing with a new member, but eventually said, "Send him to the farm, or something. It doesn't really matter. But more importantly, when he shows up, tell Jackson to stay here with everyone else. He's going to miss the meeting in City Park, but maybe he can be of some use to all of you."

Charles didn't wait for a response, he circled the building and went through the doors of the temple, and found Vincent in the rows of people sitting on the floor. He tapped him lightly on the shoulder. "Brother Vincent. Brother Vincent."

The man's trance was broken with a startle. He quickly got to his feet, before he even knew what was going on. "Yes? What is it?"

"Nice lotus. And I want you with Brother Emerson, in the control station. I know it's not your shift, but I want you watching over it. I just sent out the attack on the Karma Chip factory. You're going to start the thing with the Rehabilitation clinic. And after you get that going, you're going to get absolutely everyone armed, on the farm and in the temple, and you're going to wait on my word. You might have to leave a few people behind at the farm—they just brought in a damn new recruit, and someone's going to have to watch over him, make sure he doesn't run away. I'm going to meet all the ghosts that are still in the city, it can't wait. If any more ghosts bring any more recruits, tell them to stop, and to accompany all of you on the next phase. There will be no more recruiting for a while. And tell my engineers to just go somewhere safe and wait, they're not fighting. But give them weapons anyway, just in case. Got it?"

"Yeah, I do. I'll get right on it."

"Good."

Damon had been walking for nearly two days, his head a con-
stant explosion. For a while they had hitched a ride on a subway, but that was only for part of the way, and apparently they
weren't supposed to. Jackson had threatened him with death if
he ever told anyone.

He kept touching his ear, even though it sent waves of pain
through his entire body every time that he did. They had taken
off his ear, the whole thing, and then put it back. They tun-
neled into his brain. He could feel the sensation of the machine in his head still, tunneling from his ear, along the inside
perimeter of his skull, a few inches back to his Karma Chip.
It was still numb, but pulsing, and he couldn't stop thinking
about it.

"Why did you take my ear off?" he stammered.

"We told you that already," Jackson said patiently, as they
trudged along, nearly at the mansion.

It would have been almost tolerable, Damon thought, except that he had seen it, he had seen it happening. He had a
mirror on the inside of his bathroom door, from which he
could see himself standing in the shower. And he'd never
loved the mirror there, but he never thought that it would ruin
his life either. He was conscious when they did it, he could see
the unnatural machine, suspended above his head, a drill in his
mind, his ear off to the side, just suspended there. It was the
image. And then they just attached it again like nothing ever
happened, and there was his Chip, bloody and on the counter.
And only then did his body grant him reprieve, only then did
he pass out.

Damon was surprised when they simply went around the mansion, into the field behind it. They walked close under the building, as if they were avoiding being seen from the windows, if they could. He hoped they weren't breaking in to it. He had been doubting for quite some time if he had made the right decision—he should have just went to one of the Rehabilitation clinics and prayed for the best. He didn't know what he had signed up for. It was possible that the ear was just the beginning, that a sick, demented half-existence of being tortured lay ahead of him. It was possible that his new companions were part of the Government as well, punishing those who tried to escape their fate. The possibilities and the pain, they filled his head.

They walked through some trees, and suddenly they were in a hidden, little village, with tents and a small, wooden building. It didn't really make sense. They brought him around the back of the building, to a guy that was sitting behind a bunch of screens.

"Brother Emerson. Here he is, that new recruit I told you about. His name is Damon. Should I put him in a tent?"

"Brother Charles said to put him on the farm."

"He hasn't exactly healed yet, why aren't we putting him into a tent?"

"That was an order from Brother Charles, are you going to disobey it?"

"No, I'm not. If you say so, then. But is he around to talk to, Brother Charles?"

"He's not, he went back into the city. To the Park. He's having a meeting there with the ghosts, and he says it can't wait. He said that you should wait here, and go with all of us."

"Damn it," Jackson said, thinking about how tired he was from the long trek. "I'm not just going to wait here, if things are happening already. I'm going to that meeting."

"You couldn't possible make it in time."

"I can if I take a subway."

"You know that's dangerous, Brother Jackson," Emerson said with a frown.

"Don't even get me started. You think I don't know what's dangerous? I'm out there every day, avoiding Karma, while you sit behind these little computers, safe and sound. Don't even start. Come on, Damon, I'm taking you to the farm, where you're going to have a lot of fun, okay?"

He grabbed the disoriented man by the arm and led him out of the building. Before he had gotten very far, he told one of his group, "Go get us some of those Evaporation Pens they're making. I've got a bad feeling about this meeting. If he says no, take them. You, go with him. I'll take care of the recruit. I'll meet you both out front." The two left and he continued on to the farm.

"They'll tell you what to do," Jackson said, indicating people that were meandering about between the plants. Then he yelled, "New recruit!" before leaving Damon standing there.

It was the saddest farm that Damon had seen in his life. He'd seen pictures before, of the Government farms, vast tracks of land that had Solar Umbrellas to give them light, high-yield fertilizer, and large, intricate water sprinklers. Those plants had looked robust, healthy, fertile.

In contrast, everything on the field around him was tragically withered, bending unhealthily under the weight of the small amount of fruit that they did occasionally produce.

"This is the farm, our pride and joy," a man said, approaching Damon with a smile. "I'll show you the animals too, to give you a full tour." The man led him down a short path, down to a small field that smelled strongly of manure.

Ranging out among the weeds were a bunch of anorexic farm animals, including the thinnest pig Damon had ever seen. The cows all looked sallow as well, an unnatural yellow color that he had never expected to see. Their coloration made them look like some other animal entirely, so that he almost didn't recognize them for what they were.

"They probably haven't told you much yet, but this is what you're going to live off of, for the rest of the time you spend with the Order, so you better put everything you got into it. We only survive if we work together, and we're only working together when everyone's pulling their weight, okay? I'm going to take you back to the fields, and I'm going to get you a shovel. We're moving some manure onto the plants. It might sound gross, but I promise you that eventually you'll realize it's the most satisfying thing you've ever done."

Damon's head began to radiate pain anew, and he couldn't tell if it was because of the fresh tunnel in his brain, or the thought of working on that farm.

Charles was sitting on the same bench in the City Park that he always did, waiting. Peril, his doppelgänger, was nearby, standing immediately outside of the Privacy Room, where the Park ended. In order to guarantee the message was received, Peril was still just staring at his leather gloves, waiting for the ghosts to show up.

A lot of thoughts were going through Charles' head. He

hadn't had enough time to cultivate a stronger image. He wasn't quite sure that he had enough men for what he intended to do. The men that had attacked the Karma Chip factory, and the men that would attack the Rehabilitation clinic, were fortunately not his own. They were connections he had been lucky to make early on, people that he had hired using part of his fortune. It had always worried him that somehow that part of his plan wouldn't work, even though a lot of precautions had been taken during the transactions. He had always felt that somehow it would be discovered and traced back to him before its implementation, or that the man he paid would have just taken the money and never delivered. But it worked, or at least the first part had.

The rest of the men would be his own, moving forward. He trusted no one else. But he had no idea how many of his ghosts would show up. It was entirely a function of how many of them were checking in regularly on his Card, like they were supposed to do. He imagined that a lot of them were consistent about it—the ones that he had seen since the escalation of events, he had told to follow the guidelines closer than they ever had before. They were prone to listen, he felt.

Jackson and his men were the first to show up. Charles was somewhat confused. "How did you get here so quickly?"

"You made it sound important," Jackson said, "so we took a subway."

"How on earth did you do that?"

"That's a secret of the trade, Brother Charles."

"If you say so. I just can't have any police officers showing up to this meeting of ours."

"They won't. Not because of us, at least."

Soon more began to trickle in, and Charles began to worry about how conspicuous they would be. They had only had one other similar meeting, and it had caused quite a few people to stare, which was attention that he never wanted. "Only group leaders," he said. "The rest of you go take a walk around the Park, or something."

Before long there was fifteen of them gathered there, almost more than he had hoped for. He signaled for Peril to come back and join them, which he did.

"The plan is in its last phase," Charles said. "No more recruiting. Put your Chip removal machines somewhere where they won't be a hindrance to you. Make a quick visit to checkpoint beta, and get yourselves armed. We'll be moving in from the Monastery shortly. This will be the gathering point for you, just like we planned. Chances are, I might not be here to meet you, but you move on with or without me, tomorrow, noon, World Time. The station is down the road. Is that clear to everyone? You ghosts are one of my best assets, you know what it means to avoid Karma better than anyone. Can I count on you?"

There was a general muttering of affirmation from the crowd.

"Good, very good."

One of them suddenly spoke up, his eyes gazing off into the distance behind them. "Guys," he said. "Those are police officers. They're headed straight this way."

"Jackson," Charles said, angry. "You said it was going to be alright."

"I can promise you, Brother Charles, they're not here because of me."

"How can you promise that?"

Before he had a chance to respond, a searing beam cut through their midst, hitting no one, but splitting the ground apart between them.

"They're firing? They're actually firing at us?"

"Just run!" Charles yelled, over the confusion. "The plan is the same. Split up."

As they diffused, more beams rained down upon them, and Helicars were hovering overhead.

11

WILL WAS STANDING alone in the green light of Karma's room. "I thought you said we wouldn't be meeting again," he said, trying to lighten the mood, since he was pretty confident that he was going to die.

"Will Spector. Tell me everything you know about Charles Darcy," Karma said in its deep, inhuman voice.

"You know everything that I know. Can't you just go through my past, or something?"

"Perhaps I misspoke. You said that you saw a person without a Chip. But he was Evaporated, so we cannot find out how that's possible. Before you said it, I had not even considered the possibility."

"How is that you didn't think… you had to have known, didn't you?"

"I might have underestimated the human capacity for subversion. I'm still having difficulty comprehending why the system I've created hasn't been better received, especially considering that it is an economic necessity due to the present extensive exhaustion of Earth's resources. And I knew that there were certain isolated outbreaks of dissention, all of which I have had disposed of, but I never had cause to think that the removal of the Karma Chip was possible to survive, as this would require a high level of surgical skill, and more than one person, and a conspicuous amount of tools, all of which I have in fact been keeping track of.

"Upon the recommendation you provided at the Karma Chip factory, I started going through my files, this time looking for people that were being perceived, but not broadcasting their own signal. This calculation will take some time to make, due to the amount of people involved and the large span of time, but I've already produced a few results. They do exist. But more pertinently, I am asking you now about Charles Darcy, and your claim that he was somehow related to the attack made on my factory. How did you make this connection?"

"I was watching him on the Karma Map, and he was saying something to someone at a restaurant about a delivery of uniforms. And the people that attacked the factory were wearing uniforms. It seemed like more than a coincidence to me. And there have been other things, like a reflection of his I saw in a mirror that didn't look right. I didn't suspect a thing until Eric mentioned it, but when he did I looked into it, and I think he's right."

"Those are leaps of judgment I would have never made. I see no direct causality between the uniforms mentioned in the restaurant, and those worn at the attack. I am looking now at the reflection you describe, in the window of the subway, and I do not see anything wrong. Tell me more about this reflection."

Will wasn't quite sure if he was currently digging his own grave. Karma must have known that his heart was racing, and that he was extremely nervous. But he didn't think he could avoid the question, so he answered it directly. "I think that, somehow, more than one person is being Charles Darcy. And that is how he's got his fortune. Or at least that explains part of it. I've been in his house, and I don't know how he afforded even half of it. Have you really... not looked into that?"

"These Privacy Rooms have been a hindrance to me for a long time. I'm deactivating all of them as we speak. And as of this moment, I'm making you first in command."

"Are you serious? How is that possible?"

Karma ignored him. "Now tell me, how large of a threat do you imagine we are facing right now? What do you estimate Charles' forces to be?"

"I have no reason to believe—"

"I didn't bring you here for your reasons, do you understand? Make a guess, use your intuition, and let us address this problem."

He thought for a second. "Well I've been thinking about it for a while now, ever since I saw what I believe I saw on my Karma Map, and I'm even more convinced since I got shot by that invisible guy at the factory. Let's say that he has a way to take Karma Cards safely out of people's heads. And to put them back in, even, otherwise he could never go back to being himself. That means he has something that can switch them.

"What doesn't make sense to me is why he would draw so much attention to himself, by buying such a large house, appearing on television, all the things he's done. He has such a large secret, and yet he's drawing attention to himself, like he wants to be discovered. Although, he does have an aversion to mirrors, which is smart for a man in his position. He's at least biding time." Will became more confident as he spoke, talking quicker and taking larger leaps of deduction.

"Now if he's taking such a large risk exposing himself, I

don't see why he wouldn't take the much smaller risk of using all the faceless people you've never heard of, like the guy that just holds the door open for people that no one would remember from one day to the next. He's got the machine, so why not? Let's say he's having them do the same thing he's doing, earning more money than a person reasonably could, and all of the extra money goes to himself. There's no saying how large of an empire he could build out of that, but it could be massive, it could be thousands of people. And half of them look similar to the other half, they're trading off, leaving one invisible and one earning money. And these invisible people are doing all the secret organization stuff.

"But that would mean one of the Chips would have to be gotten rid of, and I don't know how they would do that. Fake a death or something. Is that possible? Either way, they've done it at least once with Charles, and I feel like that means they can and have done it again. Or it's possible he somehow finds kids before they grow up and get their Chip, and takes them in, raises them, brainwashes them into helping him out. Is that possible?"

"All reported children that did not die before fourteen have been given a Chip, no exceptions. I have kept track of that closely."

"Either way, if they were kids or if they were adults, these people would have had to disappear from your radar at some point. So it's nearly the same.

"Well anyway, if I were you, I'd be looking for people that are earning more money than average, that look like people that have died somehow in the past. Faces that don't match what they should when they pass the window on a building, a puddle of water on the ground, something like that. Is there any way to see who's been mentioning his name lately? I feel like if he's doing so much secret business underground, someone's going to have slipped, and said his name when they shouldn't." He was making up half of it as he went, but it felt right.

Karma responded, "Surely you must know how many people have been talking about Charles Darcy lately. I can try, but all of those computations will take time. I will get you a list of names shortly, of people that are suspect and to be apprehended. At this very moment, another attack is being led against a Rehabilitation clinic. I will send officers to counter that threat. But Charles isn't there, he's at the City Park. You are going to go to the City Park, and Evaporate Charles Darcy. I don't care what it costs. Come back right after you do it. Will you require anything?"

"I've been shot three times, does it have to be right now?"

"I will find someone else. I asked you first, because I trust you. Should I find someone else?"

Will thought it over for a couple seconds before conceding. It had to be him. "I will do it. But I'm going to need some painkillers. And a weapon with a longer range. I've been using my Grappling Chain kind of improperly to compensate for that, but it only works so well. And I want my group of people, I want Eric, Marcus, Steve and John. With long range weapons. And Helicars. And maybe twenty other people at my disposal."

"I will extend the range of your Evaporation Pen to one hundred feet, for you and the other four you mentioned. And I will have twenty people and Helicars dispatched to the roof

within five minutes, on the condition that it is never mentioned to them that Charles Darcy is your target. Your medica-
tion will be with them. Is that all?"

"Why can't I tell them he's the target?"

"I made the mistake of presenting him as a model to the
public. It would be counterproductive for them to find out
that he is a traitor. Tell the same thing to the other four that
know of your suspicion, should they ask."

"You don't want Charles alive, to interrogate?"

"Evaporate him, and everyone that follows him."

In the back of Karma's mind, it was going through all of the
dead faces that it knew, and trying to find them in other people's perspectives. The ones it thought matched, it kept separate, and constantly compared those to people that did Good
Works at a high rate. He looked through conversations and
other people's eyes, to see who was saying Charles Darcy's
name, and also who was seeing him, and when, and where.

But at the front of Karma's mind, all it could think of was
Charles Darcy himself. How could it have missed such a large
threat to itself, if what Will Spector said was true? It did not
seem possible. It must have somehow happened in the gaps of
the Privacy Rooms, but those were finally gone. Still, it did not
compensate for the past. He shouldn't have let them persist
for so long, the Privacy Rooms. If the humans demanded that
they be reinstated, Karma could always lie to them, next time.

Karma went through Charles Darcy's whole life, in a matter of seconds. Did Charles Darcy start planning everything
before he was fourteen? Karma had always wanted the Chip
to be installed earlier, but the human brain was still too unde-

veloped and erratic until fourteen for only one Chip to suffice, they would have had to go back and get it replaced every year or so and Karma knew they would object. If humans could just come out of the womb with fully developed brains, it would have solved a lot of Karma's problems. Or if Karma could raise the children itself, but the humans would object to that as well. Karma would fix it somehow.

Karma wanted to see Charles Darcy's dreams, but they didn't exist, at least not recent ones. The humans always gave themselves away the most in their dreams. Dreams were sensory impulses, as incoherent as they were, so they belonged to Karma. If he had Charles Darcy's dreams, he could have solved it himself, but the man claimed to not sleep. He used to. It was two years before that he stopped. That number had to mean something.

When he was younger, Charles Darcy dreamed of pleasant things, for humans. Of beaches, and trees, and rivers. He had dreams characteristic of an intelligent person, from the day his Chip had been inserted onward. None of the dreams ever expressed an intent to be subversive, to remove Karma Chips, or destroy factories, not even the most recent dreams, two years prior. The colors of his dreams, the shades and the nature of the people that populated them, were all from a warmer palette. At least the dreams Karma could see.

In the beginning, Karma hadn't been very good at dream interpretation, but it had read Freud, and it had spent a lot of time finding correlations between the billions of dreams he had access to, and the people's lives that they corresponded to. Once again, the Privacy Rooms prevented Karma from developing it into a science, since most people only slept outside of them on accident, but Karma was finally in a position to complete that project as well.

Karma also went through the man's finances. The house had in fact been bought by Charles Darcy himself, on the strength of the Good Works perceived by his Karma Chip. But he had bought none of the decorations in his house, none of the suits he wore, none of the little supplies that the humans needed to survive, like toothbrushes, which cost most of the humans more than they thought it did, in the long run. He only rarely bought food, even.

Karma should have noticed. Food consumption was going on the list of things to check, for the future. Karma had never thought that people using less things, being more efficient, was a sign of subversion. Until then he had thought that Charles Darcy's frugality was laudable, that Charles understood all of the things that Karma wanted all the people to understand. He had been wrong.

A list of possible traitors was already forming in the back of Karma's mind. And, out in the world, Will Spector was closing in on Charles Darcy, flying in a Helicar over the abysmal City Park. Karma would win. Karma was sure of it.

Will was sitting in a Helicar, the pain slowly evaporating from the bullet holes in his skin. Medicine was a miraculous thing. The Helicar was high above the city, making its way without deviation to the City Park. In his Helicar were four other officers he had never met, wearing helmets and holding their Grappling Chains, ready for orders. Before they had gotten onto the Helicars, Will had taken Eric and the others from their group aside and explained the situation.

"It's only us that know?" Marcus asked. "What do the other officers here think that we're doing?"

"It was Karma's orders that only we should know. They just know that we have a target to Evaporate. They only have a Card number, not a name. It's also possible that there will be more people with Charles, and we'll have to take them out too. Anyone that looks suspicious at all, we have to Evaporate."

"We're just Evaporating them, not arresting? Since when?" Marcus continued.

Will replied, "These are orders from Karma, and there's nothing more to it. We have to contain this threat. There's a lot of things going on right now, and we have to stop it before it gets out of hand, no matter what it takes."

"I understand," Eric said. "I've been watching the things happening at the Rehabilitation clinic, and this is really the biggest threat to our society I've ever head of, at least since I was born. We have to do what we have to do, as officers."

"Then let's go," Will said. "We don't have much time to spare."

And then Will was nearly there, he could see the distant spots of greyish green that appeared between tall buildings, which indicated the City Park. Will was deathly afraid of Karma, and letting it down. He had the deepest conviction that whatever Karma asked for, it was right, and he was concerned that he would not succeed. An intelligent man like Charles belonged in the Government, doing his part to peacefully make the world a better place, but instead he had deviated somewhere, and the thought disgusted Will. It disgusted him that someone like Charles had been paid for Good Works, even became rich from them, and none of them had been sincere.

The more Will thought about it, the more he wanted to Evaporate Charles.

He changed the range of his Evaporator from five to one hundred feet. He looked at his Karma Map, and could see pictured in the screen a group of fifteen people, with the audacity to have a subversive meeting in a public park, no less. He would Evaporate them all.

When they came into range, he took the first shot, aiming at the center of the group. From the corner of his eye, leaning out from the other Helicars, he could see Eric and the others doing the same.

12

FOR NEARLY A week, Aaron had been making a circuit around the city's bars, finding ones that would serve him instead of reminding him about the Tax. They always gave him one or two drinks and then became philanthropists, so he would stand up, walk to the next bar, and have his next drink or two, before continuing his cycle. Even drinking was starting to seem like a chore to him, because he had to develop a system just to do it, but it had the benefit of being entirely unrewarding, which was all that he was looking for. His credit was the lowest it had been since he had gotten the Card, and it made him smile whenever he looked at it, stumbling through the dark, thankless streets of New York City.

There was one bar he had been in, three days earlier, when a cop had shown up looking for him. He had been sitting at the counter, deprived of a third drink, and had decided to watch the television for a little bit before moving on, just to see what the world looked like for a second. The cop sat down next to him, and inspected his face.

"Can I help you, sir? You're staring," Aaron said, not looking away from the television.

"Are you an Aaron Fawley?"

"Only until I can find out how to stop."

"That isn't funny, Aaron. You, exactly as you are, have a lot to offer this society. You just need to change directions a little. My name is Will Spector."

The man had stuck out his hand, and even though Aaron passionately hated him already, he took the hand and shook it. He should have wiped his own hand first though, he realized. It was just beer, only beer, or maybe condensation, but it was still embarrassing to shake with a wet hand. A complete mistake. But it served the officer right, shaking a stranger's hands without warning. He watched Will discreetly wipe his hand on his pant leg afterward, and smiled to himself.

Aaron continued the conversation of his own accord. "My next stop is Lucky Joe's, down the road. What possible better direction is there than that."

"You could go back to doing Good Works, Aaron. I would highly recommend that. I've seen the Rehabilitation clinics myself, for the first time just only the other day, and I can promise you that you won't like them. I didn't. I'm being more honest with you than I'm supposed to, because I care. I'm supposed to just tell you that you'll go to a Rehabilitation clinic at your current rate, and let you make the decision, so that we can tell you that you were fairly warned. But I'm telling you personally that you don't want to go."

"I've always wondered what they looked like, those Rehabilitation clinics. Government doesn't tell you much, other than that's where you go to get fixed when you're broken," Aaron said, and laughed. "Did you say only recently? Are you new?"

"I am, yes," Will said.

"No wonder you're so damn perky. And what was it you did, to become a cop?"

"A lot of Good Works," Will said patiently.

"That's not what I meant, and you know it. I know how this system works. You did one thing in particular, something they could put in the newspaper so that everyone in the world knows that every cop is a complete and utter hero, so that if I complain about you being an asshole they can roll out an article and say, 'Does this look like an asshole to you? You're the asshole.' Now I'm asking you, what did you do?"

Will seemed like he wasn't going to play along, but then he rolled up the legs of his pants and showed Aaron his mechanical legs. "I got hit by a subway," he said. "Saving a kid. I used to be prettier."

"We all did, but that was yesterday. Why'd you do it? Why did you give up on the things that made you pretty, by standing in front of a subway?"

"I didn't give up on being pretty, I said I was prettier."

"Which means that you gave up at least one unit of prettiness, doesn't it? Are we talking the same language here?"

Will breathed in, breathed out. "The things that make us pretty, they aren't body parts. If I could do it all over again, I would willingly make the same sacrifice, even if there was no reward. I would give anything, if I knew that the benefit to the world was greater than the cost. Don't get me wrong, don't think that I did it all to be a police officer."

"I never said that you did it all just to be a police officer. But now that you're acting all defensive, I don't believe you."

"How did we get so off track? I'm here to tell you to get out of this bar, and back into the world. Let's go back to that."

"Whatever you want to talk about, captain, I'm all ears. You pick the topic. But I'm not leaving this bar. Or I am, but only to go to another bar because I have to. You can tell me more stories over there if you want."

"You're not taking me seriously."

"You know," Aaron said, changing his tone from sarcasm to something approaching serious. "I almost feel the exact same way that you do. All of the things you said make sense. I want to see the world going in the right direction, getting better. I would make the same trade. Where we differ, I imagine, is on our opinion on Good Works."

"If you make any heretical statements, I'll arrest you right here."

"Way to end the conversation before it began, Mr. Officer. That's why I'm just quitting, right there. It's people like you. I'll never convince you, you're far too engrained, and the only reason I could possibly think of to stick around is to convince people like you that you're all complete idiots, at least where it counts. Will you agree that you're a complete idiot?"

"Why would I do that?"

"There you have it. I'm going to the next bar. Shake? Shake hands again? Come on."

Two days later, at another bar, Aaron had been approached by another man. Before he had turned to look at him, Aaron thought it would be another cop, and that maybe it was time for him to find a better diversion. But it wasn't, it was a man that looked nearly as dirty and unemployable as himself, which surprised him.

"I've seen you here several times, man. Always drinking. And I've heard them saying you're not going to afford the Tax here coming up," the stranger said.

"Are you going to lecture me too? I've had about enough of it, so watch out."

"No, not at all, wouldn't dream of lecturing anybody on anything. But I do have something I'd like to talk to you about, if you'd join me at that booth in the corner over there." The man indicated a booth immersed in the deep gloom of the corner of the bar. "I'll be over there. Any point you think you want to hear what I have to say, you'll find me over there. For today, that is."

More curious than anything, Aaron stood up after finishing his drink, and moved over to the booth. The man was there waiting for him, a wary smile on his face.

"What is it, then?" Aaron asked, somewhat rudely.

"I'm putting myself at a lot of personal risk, offering what I'm offering, so you got to promise not to go reporting me to the police or anything. Can you promise me that?"

"Just say it already."

"Promise me."

"What does my promise to you really mean? Fine, I promise you. Now what is it?"

"I have a way of getting around the Tax," the man said, extremely quietly and looking carefully back and forth across the bar while he did.

"And what is that?"

"I can't tell you anything about it, really. I can just promise you that if you take the offer, you won't be going to any Rehabilitation clinic. And you won't have to pay the Tax."

"How am I supposed to believe that, if you can't tell me anything about it? Your promise doesn't mean anything to me either."

The man simply smiled. "Have it your way. You just looked like you could use some help. Have a good day then," he said as he stood up, and began to walk away.

"Hey, no, wait. Tell me what I would have to do."

The man sat back down. "Simple, really. You just have to say yes, and to give up on your life as you know it. I can tell you that much. But it looks like you've already done the giving up part, so all that's left is the saying yes. You don't have any family, do you?"

Aaron thought about it silently for a long time, and about Sam. "I can think about it, right? And get back to you on that?"

"That's the thing about these offers, friend, is that they're hard to keep open. I'll tell you what I can do for you, I can give you three days. For the next three days, you're going to think about it. And before those three days are up, if you decide you want to, you're going to write a letter saying yes, and your signature, and you're going to leave it under that chair you're sitting in. Pencil and paper. And then four days after that, we'll find you. That's what I can offer you, and if you let those three days go by we won't be talking again."

"Alright, I understand. I'll think about it."

The other man left the bar first, in a hurry, leaving Aaron to sit alone and think.

Around three o'clock in the afternoon, Aaron's wife was always sitting along the edge of the City Park, where Good Works still counted, folding newspapers into paper animals for the passing children. She had been so delighted when she found out that it was rewarded, even if it was only a small amount. She had said to Aaron, "It's not even work at all, and the children love it. You should see their faces, they really do love it."

Since he knew that she would be there, away from the

apartment, Aaron took the opportunity to go back and get a pencil and a few pieces of paper, and to change clothes for the first time in a week before leaving once more.

"I smell like a human again," he said to himself, after he had changed. "It's magical."

He found a café overlooking the pathetic City Park, and without buying anything at all he took a seat by a window. The prices at the café were exorbitant, since everything they served was considered a luxury. Twice he had to turn away an employee trying to get him to buy something, saying that he was still thinking about his order.

He was writing a letter. For a long time, he just sat there with a pencil in his mouth, staring blankly at the empty white pages, but eventually he took the pencil from his mouth and wrote:

Dear Sam,

Years from now, you're going to look at this letter and it's going to make you laugh. It will be our last little private joke, me and you. If you ever get a refrigerator, I want you to hang this on it, ok? You'll get a refrigerator, I know you will. You have such a kind heart, deep down. I still believe. And kind hearts deserve refrigerators.

I'm sitting here at a café I'll never be able to afford, writing this. There's a window down into the Park, and I swear I can see you, but you're so small from here. You're smiling, I know. I don't think I'm coming home again. That's probably going to upset you for a while.

I never stopped believing in the things you wanted me to believe in, I promise. I'm still in love with us, but mostly you. And I still think it's our happiness and our happiness alone that is important in this universe, but mostly yours. It's just that I'm going to bring us both down if you let me, and you will let me, so I'm going to spare you myself. I'm just not strong enough to do it face to face, so I'm using this paper. Forgive me for that, among other things.

I know that me leaving puts you in a bad place. There are bills you won't be able to pay, and you'll have to live somewhere else. But believe me when I say that this world is made for people like you, it was made specifically so that you'll always be able to get back up when you've fallen. But it doesn't work that way for me, I won't be getting back up.

I'll be leaving all my things behind. You should sell them. Sorry for the chore.

You'll probably want a reason, one that would actually convince you. I probably don't have any of those. I will say that, for a while now, I've been finding myself thinking about what is right. In a really general sense. Like, is it right to hate absolutely everyone? Probably not, but why can't it be, and who's judging? I don't believe in God, and I don't believe in karma, I don't believe in any of the things that you do, so I'm lacking a lot of motivation that you've always had an easy time finding, even if you've doubted the same things from time to time yourself.

There's nothing but ourselves, is what I've distilled it all down to, and even then, even when that's all I'm considering, I'm still doing wrong. Which is discomforting. I'm going to do it right. I've thought a lot about what that means, and this is what I've decided. You won't agree, but I know I'm right. When you read this years from now, hanging on your fridge, while you're laughing, you'll finally agree with me. You'll have filled your life with other things and you'll realize that they suit you much better. I hope you can thank me then, even when you hate me now.

Be happy.

None of it sounded right, but he put the pencil down anyway. He was done with the eraser, done with the lead. Rowing in Eden. He folded the letter up, put it into his pocket, and left.

13

NIGHT WAS CLOSING in, and Will was flying in a Helicar, on his way back to Charles' mansion. An almost beautiful, argyle sunset was happening in the distance, entirely shades of purple, a rare display of color by the sky. Sitting with him were Eric and the others. Their Evaporation Pens were being recharged in the cockpit.

Even though Charles' Karma Chip was no longer broadcasting a signal, Will wasn't sure how much that meant. It could have been his imposter that was killed—Will hadn't been close enough to see. He had taken most of his shots at the group from the height of the Helicar, only using his Grappling Chain to reach the ground when he realized that the remnants of the enemy group would need to be chased on foot.

He had chased a man down into the subway system, in the middle of a large crowd waiting for the train. The man had tried to get away by jumping onto the tracks and running through the tunnels, but Will had caught up with him in time to Evaporate him from the platform. The extended range of his Evaporation Pen was working quite well to his advantage already.

He had then gone back to Karma, who told him to go immediately back to the mansion to investigate, with Eric and the rest, and to kill whoever they might find. Will was personally carrying a large amount of explosives, with which he intended to blow the whole thing up after they were through.

If anyone was still at the mansion, they didn't have Karma Chips. To Will it didn't make much of a difference, since he had only been an officer for a short period of time, and was used to not knowing where and when people might appear. But to a cop like Eric, who was quite accustomed to the Karma Map, it must have been unsettling to be up against an unseen enemy.

Presently, Eric was talking to Will, as they waited to arrive at the mansion. "It's a really interesting time you picked to become a cop, kid. As long as I've been with the Government, I've never dealt with anything even nearly this exciting. I hope this doesn't set your expectations too high for the rest of your career, because you're going to be disappointed."

Will was curious. "What's the most exciting thing you've dealt with? Before this?"

Eric took a moment to consider. "Like I said, nothing compares. But there was this one time, I'll tell you about that. Usually, when people are trying to take out their Karma Chip on their own, they do it in their bathroom. We don't tell them they have a time limit in there before they're investigated, right? So all things being equal, they think it's best to have running water, lots of light, and a mess that's easy to clean up even though they won't be living there anymore. It's habit more than anything, really.

"But these people I'm talking about, they were a couple. And instead of going to the bathroom, they were trying to take their Chips out in their bedroom. Which gave them a lot of extra time—I almost feel like they must have known somehow. After about sixteen hours, Karma gets suspicious and sends me in. And it's one of the first calls I'd done on my own, so I'm nervous as it is.

"I walk in, go to the bedroom. Blood everywhere, disgusting. I feel like vomiting, completely nauseous. They're both still alive, the girl had been trying to take the guy's out first, and then they were going to switch, I guess. He wasn't looking too healthy, had lost a lot of blood, and she still hadn't gotten very far into his head. I'm surprised she made it as far as she did—she was either not squeamish at all, or absolutely hated the guy, I'm still not sure which. Besides probably being exhausted and frustrated, she's still pretty healthy by the time I show up.

"So I walk in, take a look. Tell them what I'm there for, and that they're committing a crime. But I'm confused by the whole thing. I'm supposed to stand somewhere that Karma can see me Evaporate them, but they're in the bedroom, and they're on the far side, which was more like ten feet, twice my range. Even more than that, I'm not actually sure the girl committed a felony, because even though she was helping him with his, hers was perfectly intact. I wanted to talk to someone before I did anything, and I didn't want them to go anywhere.

"We only get two pairs of handcuffs as officers, right? The high-torsion, and the normal. So naturally, out of propriety, even though he's not looking too hot, I put the high-torsion on him, and cuff him to the bedframe. I go to put the regular ones on her, and she's looking pretty docile so I've got my guard down, but as soon as I'm within arm's length she hits me in the face, and runs out into the hallway.

"I chase after her, down a staircase. Finally I get a hold of her, and I'm sorry to admit but I hit her in the head a little bit, to get my point across. Put on the handcuffs, walked with her back up the staircase. And on the other side of the hallway, I see a trail of blood leading to the elevator. I have no idea what it could be, because surely the man's already drained to kosher by now from his skull hole. But the trail leads to their apartment. I go in, and into the bedroom, and I see an entire bed halfway through a wall, with just an arm attached to it. One arm. He struggled with the handcuffs, they did that crazy twisting thing they do, and it sent both the bed and his arm through a wall. And then he walked away.

"The kicker is that I never found him. I went down the same elevator, with the girl. And onto the street outside, but then the trail ended. I look at my Karma Map, and he's not on that either. So I figure maybe she damaged his Chip after all. And because I have her, I have to give up and let him go. To this day, I don't know what happened to him.

"Just to see the expression on her face, I tell her that he got away, that he was free now, that he left her behind to save himself, and I congratulated her on her work. Not a single expression on her face, no spite, no smile. Two things I learned— there's a lot more blood in the human body than you'd ever expect, always remember that. Number two—I don't know what love is anymore. And I have a wife of my own. I always wonder if he just left her there, if he took his opportunity and ran, even though it cost him a limb, or if they had agreed all along that if they were caught, whoever could give their life for the other, would.

"I don't know whether they loved each other completely, or not at all. I Evaporated her there, on the street, in front of everyone, simply because I didn't want to know the answer at that point. And later that night, I went home to my wife, and realized the damage was already done, Evaporating the girl hadn't helped. I realized that I had all of the same doubts as before, except it was my life, not theirs.

"Perhaps that was a little more personal than you were looking for, but it's always what I think of, when I reflect back on my career as a police officer. It's the memory I will always have."

"Wow, shit," was all that Will could think to say. Hoping to lighten the mood, Will said, "What about you, Marcus?"

"I had to Evaporate a kid," Marcus said immediately. "I didn't want to. And just like Eric, my first reaction was to call it in, because I wasn't sure about the law, but didn't think it would possibly be the case that I would have to Evaporate him. And they told me to do it. The kid had waited until his parents were gone, and did it with a pair of pliers. He had just gotten it inserted, the incisions were all still fresh, he just undid the thread and peeled it all back off. I bet his anesthesia was still working, otherwise I don't understand it at all. But he spent too long doing it, so I was sent. And I Evaporated him, fourteen years old."

"What the hell," Will said. "I said exciting, not depressing. Now I'm just sad."

"Mine was exciting, it just happened to be depressing too," Eric said.

"I forgot the prompt," Marcus said. "After Eric's story, I thought we were doing depressing."

"And here I finally have a story to replace that one," Eric continued, "and I can't even tell anyone about it. Charles Darcy will always be the perfect model, whose life tragically ended too early. It's a shame, all of it. The loss of a good story, the fact that such a scumbag will forever be idolized by the world when chances are good people like us, who stopped him, will just be forgotten. I wonder how they're going to cover it all up, what they're going to say happened to him. They must be thinking about it already, wouldn't you say?"

"Does it make sense to you?" Will asked. "Why can't they just say the truth? That he turned out to be a fake. What damage could it really do? I don't see large rebellions happening, or people doubting the value of Karma, just because of that. We all know we need Karma. Well, most of us. The well-adjusted."

Eric said, "Karma forgive me for hazarding such a practical-minded guess, but here I go. It's more than just the fact that they'd be losing such a strong role model. Everyone wants to think they can get rich. It's the implications, it goes to show you that you can be evil to the core and still earn all of the money of being good. Maybe the general public wouldn't consciously reach that conclusion, but I bet a part of them, subconsciously, would realize it.

"A lot of people don't separate the Good Work from the good intention. And that's the perfect misunderstanding, that's just the way we want it. Accidental sincerity in a majority of the world is more valuable than the truth, at least as far as I'm concerned. Because the first one gives us harmony, and the second one doubt, and I feel like it's objectively the case that harmony is far more valuable, whatever its cause."

Will only considered it silently. A naïve part of him still thought that everyone, given the truth, would make the right decision, that the world was fundamentally good. But already he had found reasons to doubt that, being a police officer. Charles Darcy. He had spoken face to face with a reason to doubt.

When they finally landed, they spread out across the mansion, their team of five. They all kept their shoes on. Will went straight to the bathroom, where he had failed to find anything before. Eric went to the bedroom. Marcus was in the kitchen, looking out into the backyard, and Steve and John were elsewhere, overturning furniture and tearing tapestries from the walls.

Will wanted desperately to find what he had missed before. He tore the toilet from the floor, smashed it open with his bare hands, and threw the pieces of porcelain out the window. The glass shattered. He did the same with the cabinets, the towel rack, the porcelain tub. He broke everything into small pieces, and when he found nothing he threw it out the window. When the entire bathroom was stripped, he even tore out the drywall, but found nothing. "It's just a bathroom," he said to himself.

A voice responded. "Go to the backyard." It was Karma's voice, somehow speaking to him from within his own head.

Even though he knew, he asked, "Who is this?"

"You know, Will Spector. It's Karma. I'm tired of being in a tower, counting on others to do my work for me. Be my agent, be my body. And throw away your Karma Map, I will tell you everything you need to know. Help me with this."

As insane as it seemed to Will, he just accepted it. He asked, "What's in the backyard?"

"I don't know, and that's the problem. There are holes in my Map, gaps in my knowledge, and that's a problem. We need to fill those holes, Will Spector."

Will placed his Karma Map on the ground, crushed it with his mechanical foot, and then vaulted through the broken window. He ran to the back of the house, without a moment of hesitation. "It's hard to see," Will said, peering around into the darkness. The moon wasn't out that night. "Is this really helpful?"

"Some detail is better than nothing, and I only need a little bit of detail. Go out past those trees."

Will continued forward at a sprint, into the thick brush.

"Look around more," Karma said.

He moved his head back and forth constantly, not because he was actually looking for anything, but just so that Karma would have the images. Eventually he broke through to a clearing, in which there were tents and buildings.

"They were living here," Will said. "Hundreds of them." He went through the tents, the temple, the control station, all the way to the farm, where animals were still wandering around listlessly in the dark. "A little, isolated community. I can't believe it." And to Karma, he said, "Was there anything else you wanted to see."

"I want to see you destroy it, every piece. Use your Evaporation Pen. Then go back to the mansion, and blow it up. Be quick, I need you to do something else after all of this. I don't see anybody present, in the images you are sending. They are either gone, or hiding. Either way, this place should not exist."

Will took out his Pen, and Evaporated everything, starting at the farm. He Evaporated a cow, or at least what looked vaguely like a cow. He Evaporated the carefully tended rows of withered plants, the tents, the temple. The Evaporation Pen worked surprisingly well on inanimate objects—everything burst into the same billowing clouds of particles, no matter what it had been before. The walls of the temple were no different than the cows in the field. Until there was nothing left standing. It was exhilarating for him—for a long time, an unhealthy hatred towards Charles, and everything associated with him, had been building up inside of Will, and he was finally able to release a part of it. He could see the man's works disintegrate, with his own eyes, with Karma behind them.

He went back to the mansion when he had finished. The others were still destroying things with reckless abandon inside. "Find anything?" he asked to Steve and John, when he found them.

Karma answered for them, inside of Will's head. "They didn't."

"Are you talking to them as well?" Will asked.

"Only you. Don't tell them."

Will found Marcus, and told him that it was time to blow the mansion up and move on.

"But we haven't found anything yet," Eric objected.

"Then there's nothing to find."

"Fine. Give me some of the explosives, and I'll put them around."

Will retrieved the bag he had been carrying, from where he left it at the entrance. He gave a few small bundles to each of the others, and they placed them around the house before leaving.

They all got into the Helicar, and when they were a safe distance away, Will pressed a button on a remote that detonated them all. A large, spectral fire consumed everything, lighting up the world below them. When the light faded, there was nothing left. Will was satisfied.

The voice in his head spoke again. "I have the list, of potential suspects. People that have most likely worked for Charles Darcy at some point in their lives. I'm sending it to you now. I'm watching some of these people remove their Karma Chips from their head, as we speak, so I know for a certainty that they are more than suspects, they are criminals. I'm also sending more officers to Evaporate them, but I need you there too.

"The ones that already have their Chip out will be our responsibility, you and I. They will not be on my Map directly, but I can still see them as they pass by others. I will track them as best as I can, and you will find them and kill them. Tell your group you have something else to attend to, when we land."

As Karma was speaking, the Karma Card of everyone around rang, and they looked at what it had to say. It was all things that Will already knew, but he acted surprised.

"A huge list of people to Evaporate," Eric said. "All over the city." They all got out their Karma Maps, to look at where they would be going to find them. Eric asked Will, when he saw him just sitting there watching, "Aren't you going to look at your Map?"

Will thought about his Map, crushed on the floor of Charles' bathroom and then incinerated in the bomb blast. "I have other things to attend to," he said, even using Karma's phrasing. "We'll be going our separate ways, when we land."

"What does Karma have you doing?"

"I can't say."

"Well, damn. That's unfortunate," Eric said. "I hope we can still celebrate together, as a team, when this is all through. Don't go dying on us."

14

TWENTY MEN IN uniforms, carrying large bags, approached the main gate to a Rehabilitation clinic on the southern side of New York City. One of the guards was yelling down at them from a tower, telling them to back away, when he was shot several times. Another guard, who had been standing right behind him, pulled out his Evaporation Pen and walked to where he could see the approaching group, but before he could do anything he was shot down as well.

The twenty men quickly planted bombs at the base of the two towers adjoining the gate, then one on the gate itself, and backed up to detonate them. In the meantime a small group of guards had arrived on the tower from a staircase behind it, but they arrived only in time to participate in the explosion. The towers were engulfed in an incendiary cloud, the guards dying instantaneously. One of the towers collapsed down into itself, the other fell back into the main building, knocking a hole into the upper portion of the wall. The two pieces of the metal gate were thrown to either side, where they rested on the ground.

"Move in," their leader said. "Straight ahead."

They shot more guards that came through the front door of the building, and propped the door open. They had to blow up another door to make it from the front to the holding cells, but hadn't taken a single casualty until they tried to walk through the smoke of the former door into the room beyond, when two of their men were Evaporated in a single instant, by bright red light cutting through the clouds of smoke.

"Fall back," the leader said. "Throw the grenades."

"But that's where the prisoners are," one of the uniformed men objected.

"I said throw the grenades."

Three were thrown in, and a multitude of screams could be heard as they went off. The men poured into the main hall in the wake of the explosions, shooting guards that were lying prostrate on the ground, their bodies riddled with shrapnel. Several of the prison cells that had the misfortune of being close to the front door contained casualties of their own, orange bodies scattered across the floor.

"Find me some keys."

Several of his men started searching the bodies of the dead guards, until one of them produced a set of keys.

"Open the cells up, open all of them."

More guards were coming from the opposite end of the hall. They were still out of the range for their Evaporation Pens, but the guards tried to use them anyway, the red beam fading into nothing thirty feet before the group of attackers.

"You, open the cells. The rest of you, take them out."

The sixteen men that weren't trying to frantically open prison cells spread out across the width of the hall, and opened fire on the opposite end of the hallway. A single beam caught the left shoulder of one of them, and he screamed as his body quickly became a cloud. Eventually the beams stopped, and all that could be heard at the other end of the hall were the screams of prisoners.

The leader split the group into two halves, to guard either end of the hallway as they finished releasing prisoners. When all of the cells had been unlocked, he said to everyone in a booming voice, "Feel free to stay here, if you're enjoying yourself. But everyone that is inclined to join us will be given a gun, and we'll be going to another Rehabilitation clinic just a mile away, to free them too."

There were mutterings all up and down the hall. One prisoner said aloud, "They'll just kill us, there's no point."

"We've got a plan," the leader responded, but directed it to everyone. "The more people we have, the more likely we are to succeed. But we have to leave right now."

He didn't even wait for a response, he gestured for his men to rejoin him from down the hall, and they went back out the way they came. Already Helicars were hovering in the air, and police officers were repelling down with their Grappling Chains. He instructed his men to fire up at them as they ran. Behind them, a crowd of prisoners spilled out the building, frantic and orange.

"They shot Peril, they shot him. Evaporated. He's dead."

"You're going to have to calm down, Brother Charles. You knew the risks, and so did he. You shouldn't have called here. This conversation is being recorded." Vincent was sitting at the control station, back at the Monastery, watching over all of the monks that were out in the city. Charles was on the other end of the line, panting.

"This is an emergency. Doesn't it sound like an emergency? They're onto me, or they wouldn't have shot at me. They came in with a bunch of Helicars and shot at us with those Pens."

"I know, I saw it all."

"What do you mean you saw it? We were in the Park."

"I'm telling you I saw it. I was watching through Peril, and the feed never cut when he walked into the Park. The Privacy Room there isn't working."

"You take every single one of our monks, and get those Chips out of their heads, right this instant."

"That's insane. We wouldn't be able to keep track of any of them, and we still have until tomorrow. And there's no way they won't notice a hundred people disappearing simultaneously. Chances are they were just after you, they saw you walk into the Park, they turned the Room off, and now they think you're dead. So we're in the clear. That is, until they listen to this conversation and realize that they have to kill you again."

"I'm not taking any chances. If they can turn off one Privacy Room, they can turn them all off. They saw me with a group of people, so they'll be looking for more of us. We both know how good they are at finding people that are on the Map. Do it." Charles was concerned that if any of his monks were found, they would be interrogated, and say too much.

"If the Privacy Rooms really are down, they'll see us taking them out."

"I said do it. And get everyone and everything out of the Monastery, and on its way for tomorrow. We can't mess up the timing."

"Alright. But if this goes to hell, I just want you to remember that I think you're overreacting."

Charles handed back the phone to the woman he had taken it from, thanked her politely, and ran.

Vincent sounded the alarm from the temple. All of the people that had been training with weapons, and all of the people that had been working on the farm, gathered in front of the door to the control station, where he addressed them. There were a little over a hundred present, all told.

"I hate to say it," Vincent started, "but I think it's become time to say goodbye to our Monastery. Brother Charles is under the impression that the police are on their way here now."

Everyone began to panic, and a few began to run away.

"Whoa, hold it. I've got more things to say here, I promise I'll keep it short, okay? We need to get all of our equipment from over there, and get it to the old subway station. Checkpoint gamma. And each of you will be given one of the weapons you've been training with for a while now, just in case we get spotted. That's all I've got, so let's get going. Stay focused."

They moved in a mass to where a lot of boxes were being stored behind the temple, which was also where they had been keeping all of the reverse-engineered Evaporation Pens and Grappling Chains. Vincent helped to pass them all out, before having everyone take some of the boxes and follow him along a desolate road towards an abandoned subway station.

One of the monks was walking alongside Damon, who had only been at the farm for about an hour before the alarm had been rung and everyone was called to the temple. The monk could see the fresh cut along the outside of the man's ear, and the bewilderment in his face. He said to Damon, "You just have bad timing, man. It's not always like this. It's usually pretty relaxing, really. You just have bad timing. How long ago did they take out your Chip?"

"I haven't really woken up yet," Damon said, and looked

around the large box he was carrying, down at the Evaporation Pen and Grappling Chain that were hanging at his sides.

"Yeah, bad timing man. Well good luck." He immediately hurried off ahead, because he felt that even though he was just trying to be polite, the conversation had become awkward and he didn't want to hang around. Damon just kept plodding forward, one foot after the other. He was going back the direction he had come from only an hour before, when he had arrived, the only difference being the box in his hands and the weapons he didn't understand.

"Aren't those Helicars?" one of the monks said, pointing off into the distance. The group was going through a neighborhood of rundown houses, walking down the middle of the road.

"Damn, they are," Vincent said. "Everyone, get behind one of those houses. We can't let them see us." Quickly they scattered, and Vincent watched from around a corner as the Helicars made their way towards the mansion. "Okay, let's keep going."

Eventually they reached the old subway station. It had been deemed obsolete when the newer subway system had been installed ten years before, but it still connected to one of the lines, two miles down its tracks. They broke the chains that were around the door, and entered the empty building. Down the stairs was a dark, graffiti-filled platform. All of the benches were broken, and the electronic fixtures had all fallen down.

Vincent was talking to everyone again. "We're going to go about a mile and a half down these tracks, and we're going to stay there for the night. We're going to take shifts, guarding both sides. They're probably not going to find us here, but if they do we're going to have to put up a fight. Now let's go, let's get all these boxes off the platform and onto the tracks."

While the monks were doing that, Vincent walked back to the door of the station, and looked in the direction of the mansion. He could have sworn he could see a glow in the distance, as if they had set the place on fire. He sighed, and shut the door.

Charles had to find a place to stay for the night, without using a Karma Card and without being seen by anyone. He wasn't looking forward to it. No matter where he slept, there was the possibility that he would never wake up, that he would just be Evaporated and that would be the end of it. It struck him as ironic that 'the man who never slept' was having such a problem. Maybe, for just that night, he would live up to his reputation.

He ran his hand along his newly shaved head. He'd never had a shaved head before. There was something that felt fresh about it, although he felt that it probably didn't suit his face very well. He didn't even know—he had taken all the mirrors out of his life, so long ago that he wouldn't have even remembered what he looked like had he not seen the newspaper articles, and for Peril. For the first time since it was given to him when he was fourteen, he could feel the scar of where they'd put his Karma Chip, a little square patch behind his left ear. It was an interesting reminder to have, so close in time to what he intended to do.

He would destroy Karma. He was still terribly shaken by the loss of Peril. He had been standing right next to the man, when the beam cut through him. And then he had just run away, as fast as he could. They had repelled down from the Helicars and chased them all, but Charles had been able to lose his pursuers in an alleyway. It was entirely his own fault that Peril had died. He had been unable to deal with the burden of being himself all of the time, so he had ordered someone to share it with him. And because he was in a position of power, no one had questioned the order. And this was what it had led to.

He'd seen a lot of people die, yet Peril's death had affected him the most. It was probably because, in a strange way, he watched himself die. The man had his clothes, his hair, even his face. Inside of his head, he was carrying around his Karma Chip, his moral obligation to the world. And he had watched it all disintegrate, turn into a cloud and disappear, as simple as that. The image was haunting him, and he couldn't do anything about it.

He would be killed twice before the end of the next day, he knew. It wasn't the plan, but it was going to happen. But he would destroy Karma before that, no matter what. If he became a cloud of a person overnight, he would be a thundercloud, he would gather electricity and strike Karma from above before he ever gave up.

The most unfortunate part about his plan was that he couldn't afford to die. He was absolutely willing to die, in the name of the cause, but he couldn't. So he searched around for a safe place to stay the night, so that he would make it to the next day.

"I bet they wouldn't expect me to go back to the Park," he thought to himself. "To the place we were discovered, to the place I died. I'll be one of the homeless tonight, the kind that sleep on the benches, underneath the pollution, underneath the Solar Kite, underneath the stars. Usually they come around and clear them out, the police, but I imagine they will be busy tonight, chasing ghosts.

"That will be the full circle. Yesterday, I was the richest citizen in the world, tonight I will be the poorest. And tomorrow what will I be?"

He laughed to himself, and said aloud, "A king or a cloud. There is no in between."

15

WHEN THE HELICAR landed by the City Park, Will went his separate way from the others. He wished them all the best of luck, and ran off immediately in the direction that Karma provided him. It was around two in the morning.

When he was out of sight of the others, he could finally talk to Karma again. He had to speak aloud to be heard by Karma, which was somewhat inconvenient when he wanted to look like a normal person. Since he was alone, he asked, "Where are we going?"

"The first person will be in a bar, the Town Pump. Unless he had another way out of a room that the bartender showed him into, then he will still be there. The bartender is complicit in the crime, he will be Evaporated too."

It was two miles, but Will went entirely by foot, running. Ever since he had gotten used to his new legs, he would not have had them any other way. Besides the fact that he had to charge them once every other week, they never fatigued, and he made it to his destination in a matter of minutes. He stood at the door, waiting to go in.

"It's last call, isn't it? Will only the two of them be inside?"

"There's a whole crowd of people in there still. The bartender did not announce last call. He will be to your right, almost immediately. Eight people to your left. After you Evaporate the bartender, go to the far, back-right corner, there will be a hallway and a room to the right again. If there is a man in there, you will Evaporate him.

"I almost think I could show you, but it is much easier to add aural stimuli to your brain than it is to add visual. I'm not sure how your brain would react, and I don't think now is the best time to experiment. Maybe later."

"Okay. Maybe later." Will pushed the door open, looked to his right and left, saw all of the people for himself, and then walked to the bar.

The bartender was beginning to form words with his mouth, either to tell Will to leave or to offer him a drink, when Will Evaporated him. Some of the people standing behind him, most of whom had watched him walk in, began to scream or to run for the door. Will let them go, he went immediately for the hallway he could see in the corner, through the dim lighting of the bar.

"What are the chances he's still in there?" Will asked.

"There isn't a window," Karma replied.

Will opened the door silently. A man was sleeping on a small cot, laid out in the middle of a room full of bar supplies—broken stools, kegs of beer, mop buckets. Will could hear him lightly snoring, over the commotion in the bar behind him. He Evaporated the man while he slept.

After he had done it, and while he was making his way back out of the newly empty bar, Will asked, "He really wasn't broadcasting? You couldn't see him there?"

"No. It was just probability. The exact same way that I would have to find a child, if it were necessary for me to do so. For all intents and purposes, we're hunting down children, Will

Spector. And there are quite a few more. I'm going to give you your next destination now."

"I'm listening."

The next person that Karma made him chase was nowhere to be found. It was in a restaurant that was already closed. Karma wanted one of the cooks to be Evaporated too, but he had already gone home for the night, and it would have to wait.

Will had broken through the back door, into complete darkness, and Karma had directed his steps, but it had been to no avail. The lights proved the place to be vacant. After going through the whole place, Will asked, "How long ago did you see him?"

"It was two hours ago. And I haven't seen him anywhere since—this was the last place."

"Where else should I try to look?"

"We move on. Next on the list. I can actually see five of them now, waiting for a subway, one mile away. Run south five blocks, then go west for two. You will find a subway station."

Will knocked over a few people on the way, drunk people meandering home from the bars. Half of him wanted to stop to apologize, but the other half of him realized that he had no time to spare. He tried jumping, once he was safely outside, and almost made it an entire block before landing.

"The subway has already arrived, and they're getting on it. Hurry."

He had just caught sight of the entrance down into the subterranean world of the subway. He hurdled the stairs, through a group of people who had just debarked from the same subway that he was after, just in time to see the subway leaving.

"It's gone," he told Karma.

"Go after it."

He was careful not to jump when he went from the platform to the tracks. In the controlled environment of the tunnel, which was nearly uniform as far as the eye could see, he was interested to see how fast he could actually run, if he put all of his energy into the effort. He was pleased to find that he could catch up with the subway in no time at all. He grabbed on to a railing on the back of the train, and pulled himself up.

Through a small window, he could see that no one was in the back car. Since there was no door, with his bare hand he punched through the metal wall, making perforations, until he was able to peel away a hole large enough for him to fit through. He then walked through the connecting cars, one by one, until he found the group of people.

"All of them?" he asked, while he was still sure they wouldn't hear him.

"There are five sitting there, those are them."

It seemed to Will that he could make a mistake, Evaporate an entirely wrong group of people, and Karma wouldn't mind, so long as he then went on to Evaporate the right group of people. Karma would only give him verification that his targets were right if he asked first, it seemed. To Will, the group of five that he could see, nearer to him, looked no different than a similar group further on—they were ordinary people, talking quietly, weary from the late hour.

"You said you didn't want to mess with my visual stimuli, or something like that, but from now on could you highlight the people I'm after, or something? It would make me feel better."

"That sounds possible. Let me try."

Immediately the people began to glow, an effect that Will struggled with after all, as it made him slightly dizzy. It was entirely unnatural, the way they glowed, but just like he had asked it clearly indicated that they were the ones he was after, which made him happy through the dizziness.

"Why haven't you tried this kind of thing before, with officers? It seems useful."

"I thought it was prudent to conceal the full extent of my powers. But now is a time of crisis, so an exception will be made. But only with you."

Will said nothing in response. He casually walked up to the group, like a stranger soliciting advice. Three of them looked up at him expectantly, the other two were lost in thought. As if he were looking for something he wanted to show them, he searched around in his pocket for his Evaporation Pen, smiled when his hand closed around it, and took it out. He Evaporated one of the men that was looking at him—their eyes were locked the whole time, the man didn't even know to react.

Unexpectedly, one of the men that was turned away from Will grabbed his arm, and threw him against the wall. In his surprise, his hand tensed around the trigger of the Pen, and he shot through the row of seats that were past the group.

Will's head broke a window, but he recovered quickly. With his left hand, he grabbed the wrist of the man, who was still desperately holding on to Will's right arm, the one that held the Evaporation Pen. With a simple movement, he threw the man through the window his head had broken, straight into the tunnel wall outside. Will could hear the sounds of the man being flattened against the concrete wall.

In the meantime, another had punched Will in the face. It

damaged the man's hand far more than his face. He Evaporated him, and was simultaneously shot for the fourth time in both his life and the past ten hours, by a man behind him.

"Where are they getting guns?" he asked, not concerned what the remaining men would think of him if he talked to himself, since he was confident he would kill them all.

"If I knew that, they wouldn't have them," Karma said.

Will kicked the man behind him, without looking back to aim. His leg went through the man's chest, and even though he had no nerves in his feet, the feeling sickened him tremendously.

"Don't you want one of them alive? To ask what's going on?"

"We don't have time for that. There are more after this. There are eighty-six of these people who have already removed their Chips, and we've only taken care of five of them ourselves. I have twenty seven other suspects that your friends can take care of, since they still have their Chips, but if any of them are in fact terrorists and remove their Chips before your friends find them, that will be more for us. Just keep going."

While Karma spoke, Will removed his foot from the body it was stuck in, Evaporated the last living man who had tried to escape to another car, and then Evaporated the remains of the man behind him.

"Tell me where to go, then," Will said.

The later into the morning it became, the less successful each attempt was to find Karma's targets. Will was taken all around New York City by the time dawn spread across the sky, and had Evaporated around twenty people, in streets, in bars, in apartments. Half of the time, there were other people there that watched him do it. But if they weren't highlighted in his eyes, Will ignored them, however they reacted. Some screamed, some actually attacked him, but he had arrived to a mental state where they simply seized to exist to him.

It was taking a toll on his body, the parts of him that were still real. He was much stronger than he'd ever been before, to the point that he almost considered himself inhuman, but he had run for hundreds of miles, and punched through walls, and the weariness building in his muscles and the blood that crusted his hands were still his own.

In the morning light he had become more pensive, although he still did whatever Karma told him to, wordlessly. He recalled vividly, and seemingly without reason, the first person that he had Evaporated. The man in his bathroom. He remembered how he had felt, how sick to his core he had been. He had needed Eric to help him back to the police station, where he had done nothing for the rest of the day. He had sat and stared at a ceiling, until everyone had left for the evening. And no one had bothered him.

And somehow, since then, he had become entirely at peace with the concept of Evaporation. Even more, he became at peace with himself being the hand that delivered it, as an extension of Karma's will. He wondered how that was possible, what rearrangements inside of his brain had been necessary for going from the person he had been to the person he turned into. He wondered how aware Karma had been of those changes, if Karma was even capable of guiding the transition. It occurred to him that he had no idea what Karma was capable of, although Karma's overlooking of Charles proved that perhaps a lot was out of the computer's reach.

What it amounted to, his mental reflection as his body forged onward on its own, was the closest thing to doubt that he would ever experience, in the face of Karma. "What if Karma knew everything, not just the sights and the sounds, but the thought of every person, all of the time? Would the world be a better place?" he thought. The answer didn't occur to him as obviously as it had before.

As a child, he had dreamed of being the champion of Karma, and there he was, fulfilling that dream as completely as could be hoped. If he thwarted Charles Darcy's plans, whatever they might be, he would be the champion of the century. But it wasn't what he envisioned as a child. They didn't tell children that people died for their sins—they didn't even tell the adults. They just waited for the sins to be committed, and then sent people like Will in to pay them back.

Will didn't even know who he meant by 'they'—there was no definite body from which those actions stemmed, there was only Karma. But Karma was just a computer, after all, programmed by people who thought it would be prudent for it to make decisions the way it did. "Were they right?" he asked himself. He had been abstracting the ideal of Karma from its very real origins as a product of humanity, his whole life.

His conclusion was that the abstraction could be made— that the ideal of Karma was independent of its origins. That what was right was far easier for a nearly omniscient computer to decide, than for his own limited mind. So he surrendered his belief to that computer. If he hadn't, he wouldn't have been chasing so many people down, to Evaporate them. He had no full comprehension of their sin—but he trusted that he didn't need to know, that everything was as it should be.

"You're quiet," Karma said.

"I'm doing my job," Will replied. It was ten in the morning, and he was having a hard time catching his breath. Without really being aware of it, he had Evaporated four more people.

"Do you require rest?" Karma asked.

"I might become useless to you here soon, if I don't," he said, knowing that it was true.

"Come back to Karma Tower, and sleep here. If I need you again, I will wake you."

Will was relieved, but was worried that he was letting Karma down. "Are you sure that's alright?"

"We're both practical people," Karma said. "Don't think that I'm unreasonable. We've made good progress, in these past few hours. And these humans can't hide forever—at some point, they will have to go into the world, to eat, to sleep, to live. And when they do, we will see them, and we will take care of them then."

"That's a deal," Will said.

16

CHARLES WOKE UP in the City Park, morning light around him, surprised to be alive. As uncomfortable as it had been, he had slept under a bush, hoping that no one would spot him and that he didn't snore too loud. He had started the night out on one of the park benches, but realized that if anyone at all were to see him, then that would be enough to give him away. Other than being slightly colder than he would have preferred, his health was entirely robust.

"I just have to make it to the station in time," he thought to himself. It almost didn't even matter if he was seen anymore, just as long as he made it to his destination. Silently he let the time pass by, the adrenaline in his veins making his empty stomach feel sick. People walked past, he could hear their idle conversation, but no one noticed him.

As soon as he resolved to leave as discreetly as he could, a young couple sat down on a bench ten feet away from where he was, facing him. He didn't think there was any danger of being spotted if he stayed still, but it committed him to an indefinite amount of time waiting under a bush, since he couldn't leave without making a scene. So he lay there and listened.

The young man was saying, "I don't see what the problem is. I don't care if anyone else sees. I don't care if everyone sees, everyone we know. They're all in the same situation, and they know that we do it. If you let this affect you, then how are we ever going to get past this? What if it never changes back?"

They were both mad. The man carried all of his frustration in his eyes, the girl pouted cutely, childishly. She wouldn't look him directly in the eyes as he spoke to her, as much as he kept trying to visually position himself in front of her as they sat next to each other on the bench.

She said, "We can wait. We can at least wait longer than we have. If they were going to take down the Privacy Rooms forever, they would have said so in the newspaper. They're just having technical difficulties. When they fix them, they'll tell us all it was just a glitch in the system, and that everything's good again. We'll wait until then."

"That's the stupidest thing I've ever heard," he said. "They didn't 'accidentally' turn off every Privacy Room in the entire world. They're intentionally invading our privacy. Now we have two options, we either stop doing anything private and embarrassing ever, or we redefine privacy and move on, me and you. I think it's obvious that it should be the second. You're not going to stop going to the bathroom, just because there aren't any Privacy Rooms, are you?"

"I haven't, ever since I found out that they're gone."

"Are you serious? What if this lasts even just as long as a week? You're going to hold it that long?"

"If I don't, then any one of those police, or Government officials, can pull up my file, if they feel like it, and watch me go to the bathroom. I don't think it's unreasonable that it bothers me, and I just need you to agree with me."

"But us. That does not mean that we have to stop. We can turn all the lights off, put on some music, put bags over our head, and they'll never know what's going on. For all they know, we're having a strange party. And we will be. Work with me on this. And if they figure it out, who cares."

"My parents don't know we're doing it yet," she said.

"And which one of your parents is a Government official, again? Because I forgot."

"Adam…"

Charles took pity on their situation, since it was partially his fault anyway, but he was really in a hurry, and they didn't seem like they intended to move anytime soon. So he dug out an Evaporation Pen from his breast pocket, set the range to ten feet, and Evaporated them both in one shot. Then he awkwardly climbed out of the bush, and walked quickly towards the subway station, looking to his left and right to make sure that he hadn't drawn any attention to himself.

Thirty miles away from where Charles was, the group of monks that had spent the night in an abandoned subway station was on the move. Vincent waited for the 11:20 train to go by, and when it did he had everyone pick up all of the supplies and run along behind it, as fast as they could manage with the burden they carried. They had twenty minutes to run about three miles, if they didn't want to be struck from behind, and the conditions weren't in their favor.

"I don't know which part of this plan I've always hated most," Vincent said to no one in particular as he ran. "The potential for the Monastery to be destroyed—and surely, it's destroyed by now—the fact that we're all going to die by the end of it, or the three mile run we've got to do right now. But of course it's all got to happen anyway. Charles wouldn't have it any other way."

A man running next to him, panting heavily and awkwardly nesting a box on top of his head, corrected Vincent. "Brother Charles. Brother Charles wouldn't have it any other way."

"Do you even know what the plan is, dude? Because I'm pretty sure that I'm the only one that does, and I'm telling you that it sucks."

"Brother Charles knows what's best," the monk said. "I don't need to know the details."

The simple faith of the man bothered Vincent. He had always felt the same way, that Charles probably did know best, and that it was best if he just quietly obeyed, but he had always been ashamed of that relationship, and for some reason it bothered him to hear the same logic from someone else.

"Is he really that charismatic?" Vincent thought to himself. They had met in a bar, Vincent and Charles, before the Order ever existed, and Vincent had listened to the man for hours, going on and on in an eccentric way about his ideals, and his plans for improving the human race. That was how Charles had described it—the entire human race. That was the smallest concern that the man was capable of. He didn't want to just help his family, his friends, his neighbor, not even himself. He had always talked about everyone or no one at all, and still did.

"If I spend my whole life on one Good Work, improving the life of everybody all at once, I'll never be rewarded for it. That's a fault in the system," Charles had said. "For some reason it was assumed by the people that made Karma that every worthwhile, valuable Good Work could be accomplished in less than five minutes. It literally does not consider anything that takes longer than that—I've looked at the code, and I've got a reasonable understanding of computer science to back me up.

"Five minutes. I want to do something far greater than five minutes can contain, but I'm not going to expect anything in return. Does that interest you? Do you know what I'm saying? Vincent?"

And for whatever reason, Vincent had agreed, had been entranced by the ideal. But, after running for a little over a mile, his thoughts were stagnating in his oxygen deprived brain, ideals meant nothing to him, and he wondered with what wonder he had left what he had ever been thinking.

He kept running anyway. He realized at two and a half miles, with a train audibly catching up to them from behind, that he still had yet to explain the next portion of the plan to anyone. He hated everything. "Everyone!" he yelled, and coughed mucus. "We get to station. We get out of way of hit. We get on train."

There were some people lagging behind the main group, but for the most part it looked like they would make it, to Vincent. He was glad to see that everyone was still carrying their boxes. Unknown to everyone but him, they had brought five copies of everything they needed, just in case eighty percent of them were killed or gave up.

The station opened up in front of them. Some people dropped their boxes and fell to the ground panting, still on the tracks. "You idiot!" Vincent yelled. "Did you hear me? Do you hear that? Get the hell up."

Bystanders waiting for the approaching subway looked down at them in confusion. Vincent pulled himself up onto the platform, then helped both people and boxes to be transferred up. When he was confident that he had established a system they would follow, he turned to address the crowd of people around him that were not monks.

He was still out of breath, but managed to say, so that everyone could hear, "You will not be getting on this subway, any of you. We're taking it. I suggest you all leave right now."

A burly man carrying a suitcase disagreed with Vincent. He said, "I need to get on that subway."

"You don't need to do anything, except get out of here if you want to live."

That upset the man, who didn't appreciate the threat, and he started approaching Vincent, intending to hit him. Before he made it very far, Vincent Evaporated him. "Anyone else?" Vincent yelled. The station cleared of people just as the subway arrived. He made the same threats to all of the passengers onboard, and loaded everyone and everything they had onto it, in the forty-five seconds before the doors closed and the subway continued along its route.

"What happens next?" One of the monks asked him, as they all sat down and caught their breath.

"We still have two transfers to make," Vincent said. "This subway doesn't go where we're going."

"That's not going to be easy," the monk said.

"I know. Everyone get their Evaporation Pens out, right now. Expect company."

Charles waited with a group of people for the subway to show up. The closer it came to arriving, the less cautious he was about hiding his identity from the people around him. If his monks were not on their way, then it was meaningless whether he was discovered or not.

Two minutes before the arrival of the subway, which was

always prompt, a large group of police officers joined the crowd that was forming near the platform. After looking at their Karma Maps and Cards for a brief moment, they began telling everyone to leave, while they started to set up explosives that they had brought with them. Because Charles knew that he had no other option, with a minute to spare he began Evaporating every police officer that he could see.

It wasn't terribly hard for him to take care of all of them. Their range was five feet, his was limited only by physics. He backed himself against a wall, to make sure he wasn't caught from behind, and shot anything that moved. The few bystanders that were slow to follow orders finally left, screaming.

And finally the subway arrived, which he was pleased to find full of monks. He waved at them as the doors opened, and Vincent yelled at a few of the monks that were aiming their Pens at him in anticipation. "That's one of ours. Let him on."

On the train, Charles sat next to Vincent. Across the aisle from both of them was sitting Jackson.

"Good to see you alive, Brother Jackson," Charles said.

"The same to you, Brother Charles. It was crazy there, back at the Park. If I didn't bring an Evaporation Pen with me, I wouldn't have made it."

Charles hadn't given any of his monks an Evaporation Pen, even his ghosts, because he didn't trust them enough. He had made a cost-benefit analysis, and decided it was better for a monk to die in an unpleasant, potentially avoidable situation than to give away their martial capabilities. At least until the very last stage of the plan, when it didn't matter anymore. So he didn't know where Jackson got a Pen, but he recognized that there was no point in chastising his ghost. "I know it was crazy, and I'm sorry. Brother Vincent, do we have everything?"

"In triplicate," Vincent said. "More than triplicate. And we really haven't run into too many problems. All of the police must be out there taking care of the Rehabilitation clinic rebellions, like you planned. I haven't seen any."

"They're still around. I don't know if you could tell at that last stop, but I Evaporated a whole group of them. Don't let your guard down. What's up with that guy down there? He's bleeding out of his ear." Charles indicated Damon, who was sitting with a Pen in his hand, staring blankly in front of him.

"Oh, he's new, Brother Charles," a monk sitting next to Damon said.

"Of course," Charles said, not quite understanding.

Since they only had one more stop before Karma Tower, Charles decided it was a good time to tell his plan in full to his Order, as they sped along ahead. "You've all been carrying a few things I would like to explain," Charles said. "Some of those boxes are explosives, but the more important boxes are a really large Privacy Room that we've been working on for a while. My ghosts—which I see at least some of you made it," he said, acknowledging Jackson in particular, "they're going to take four of the corners, up to the top of Karma Tower. The rest of you are going to take the four bottom corners, and some of you are going to guard them while the rest of you join me in the Tower.

"Brother Vincent will divide the duties out here in the next few minutes, I just wanted to give you an overview. It's very important that the Privacy Room is set up, and protected. Police officers may come to try to break them, if they're on to our plan. Police officers will probably try to come and kill you, whether they're on to our plan or not.

"I want to thank you for coming this far. This is nearly it. In less than thirty minutes, we'll either be complete failures or champions of justice, but either way I'm glad that we tried. It's more than most have done. And it's been an honor, being a brother to you all. It's more than just a word we use—I hope you've all found that to be true.

"Forget about probability, actually. Forget about failure. We're going to destroy Karma."

They all cheered, as he discreetly left in the direction of the front of the subway, to watch as they approached. Vincent told everyone what their duties would be as soon as they arrived.

When they reached Karma Tower, and the large group of monks split into smaller groups to do their individual tasks, Charles found the first pedestrian that he could, walking on the street in front of the building. He handed them a piece of paper, and then pointed a gun at their head. The gun was useless, but it was his experience that if he pointed an Evaporation Pen at a complete stranger, they usually just laughed at him.

"Call the number," he said.

The man he had found was nervous, but did what he was told. He brought out his Karma Card, and said to it, "Call PQ-8316."

Charles took the Card out of his hand when it began to ring. A man answered on the other end of the line.

"Marcus?" Charles asked.

"Here," Marcus replied.

"We're set over here. Are they still the only ones that know? You're with all of them?"

Marcus looked around at the other people in the Helicar

with him, as they flew out to join officers suppressing the rebellion that was still underway at one of the Rehabilitation clinics. There was Eric, Steve, John, and a few other officers that had been placed with them to fill the Helicar. Will wasn't there.

"I'm with all of them. As far as I know," he said. "Karma was pretty clear about keeping you a secret," he said.

Sitting across from him, Eric asked Marcus who he was talking to.

"Then take care of it," Charles said.

Marcus hung up the Card, and then Evaporated Steve and another officer with one shot. The sides of the Helicar were open, so he easily kicked two of the other remaining officers out of it before they had time to react, and they fell a half mile to the ground below. Then he Evaporated John as well. He wanted to save Eric for last.

Eric caught his hand, but only after he had finished Evaporating John. "What are you doing?" Eric asked, confusion in his eyes. "This shouldn't be possible. You shoot one officer, and your weapons stop working. Those are the rules."

"This Pen is homemade," Marcus said as he punched Eric in the face. Eric fell to the ground of the Helicar, still stunned. "I've always hated you the most," Marcus said, as he punched him repeatedly in the face, on the ground. Eric didn't defend himself. Evaporation was too simple for all of the resentment that Marcus had harbored against Eric for the past two years. He wanted to see the man suffer.

The pilot looked back at the two remaining men, Marcus standing, Eric lying on the ground, barely conscious. "Turn this around, and go back to Karma Tower," Marcus said. "Or I will kill you too."

17

"WILL SPECTOR, WAKE up."

Will was startled from his sleep, which it felt like he had hardly begun.

"There are people in the building."

"What do you mean?" he asked the darkness that was around him. Karma never answered—it was just the silence of his own mind, and the building around him. He looked at his Karma Card to see that he had only slept for an hour. Every one of his joints ached, and every one of his muscles. He was confused and tired.

He tried turning on a nearby Karma Map, to see if he could see any of the people that Karma meant. The Map worked, but it showed that no one was inside of the building, including himself. He was not broadcasting. And Karma wasn't talking to him. As tired as he was, he picked up all of his weapons, stepped into the hall, and picked a direction to begin looking.

The Privacy Room was set up. Charles had sent Jackson and a few other groups out ahead, and when they had everything in position and turned on, it worked just as he had hoped. He was looking over Vincent's shoulder at a Karma Map that the man was holding, and he saw exactly what he wanted to see. Nothing.

"We're clear to go in," Charles said. "Blow up the elevators behind us. And start setting up all of the explosives around the ground floor, too. I'm still not sure that we can knock it over, but if we can, all the better. Have everyone else go into the building, and kill whoever they find there. Tell them to be sure to use the stairs, and get out on time."

He took a small group of his ghosts with him, which he was sure to hand extra Evaporation Pens to. As he walked with them to the nearest elevator, he said to them, "As you all know, there's that stupid rule the officers have where if they shoot their Evaporation Pen in a Privacy Room, it automatically turns off all of their weapons afterward. But that still gives them one shot, so let's not take any chances. You see someone, you shoot. Except for Marcus, no shooting Marcus."

They got into the elevator, and he had it take them to the roof. While they went up, he continued telling them, "Any Helicars try to land on the building while we're up there, we shoot them down. I told Marcus to fly with his spotlight on, if he comes in, so that's the sign that you let that one past."

They reached the roof, and he had them spread out so they covered it from all sides. Charles hoped that he wouldn't have to wait long for Marcus to show up. When he had been on the ground, he had Vincent verify that he was on his way with a Helicar, but Charles didn't take a Karma Map with him to the roof, because he hated them. If, for some reason, Marcus didn't show up within five minutes, he would go on without him.

He leaned over the edge of the building, from a dazzling height, to see if he could make out what was going on below him. He felt the building shake lightly when the elevators were blown up, and he could see red beams on the distant ground, but he couldn't tell what was being shot at. As long as the Privacy Room remained intact, it would be alright.

A Helicar without a spotlight tried to land on the building. While it was still approaching, he shot it down himself, and its fragments collided with the side of the building, causing a slight tremor to go through it. There had been around ten men riding on it, and a few had tried jumping from it when they saw the red beam coming at them, but none of them had made it to the building. On the opposite side, he saw a similar scene unravel with another Helicar.

Then he spotted Marcus, arriving from the west. He hurried to that side of the building, just to make sure that no one shot him down when he came within range. "Marcus!" he yelled into the noise of the Helicar as it landed. "Good to see you well!"

"I'm only so well," Marcus said.

"But you took care of the people I needed you to? The people that were rooting around my mansion?"

"Yes, I did. And I brought a pilot, for the escape. We've got plenty of Helicars around here," he said, indicating the spare vehicles parked around the roof in rows, "but I figured you would want someone trained to fly one. Even though they're not that hard."

"A brilliant idea, but of course we'll have to kill him afterward."

"I've got him cuffed to the helm," Marcus said.

"Did you bring me a ship? Very nice. But let's talk about the now. Show me to Karma."

"You blew up the elevators?"

"Yes, yes I did."

"Then we'll take the stairs."

They only had to go down two flights, before reaching the floor that Karma was on. Marcus led the way, opening the doors that were locked and selecting the branches of the hallways they encountered. They reached a long hallway, the end of which couldn't be seen because of a staircase that went down at the end of it. They passed several doors, walking slowly.

"At the very least," Marcus said, "there will be two people down there."

"And how far will they be from the base of the stairs?" Charles asked.

"About twenty feet."

"This is absurdly easy," Charles said. "It's almost embarrassing. Ghosts, you go ahead, and take them out where they can't reach you. We'll be right behind."

Charles waited and listened, as he could hear blasts and sounds of human exertion below. When it became quiet, he and Marcus descended the stairs, into the room below.

He had lost a ghost somehow, but they were there, directly in front of Karma.

"This is really it?" Charles asked.

"Yes it is," Marcus said.

"And Karma's memory is kept here?"

"You know the system more than I do, you know how Karma works. I don't. But as an officer, this is the one and only place I've ever heard referred to as containing any part of Karma. This should be it."

"Well then, here we go."

"Stop there!" came a shout from the hall they had just left.

"Tell him he's too late, Brother Clinton," he said to one of the ghosts that was standing next to him. "That he shouldn't even bother. I'm going to go into this room and finish this, and we can take care of him after."

"I know that it's you, Charles," the voice said again.

"Never mind. He has my attention. That isn't that Will kid, is it? I recognize the voice. Marcus, you told me you took care of them all."

Marcus didn't respond.

"Marcus! I asked you if you could handle it, and you said that you would. Now why is he still here?"

"He wasn't around, Karma had him off doing other things," Marcus said. "And he's a good kid. He hasn't been an officer that long, he hasn't turned into an inhuman machine yet. I was hoping that he would be wise and stay away. But let's say we let him live, what's the worst he could do?"

"Marcus," Charles started. "I know that you've spent a lot of time with these people, and that you were bound to develop some attachments to some of them. I know that I'm asking a lot. But I can't have any of this. There's no room for this kind of thing. And there's especially no room for you lying to me, that's what upsets me the most. Now we're going to go deal with this right now, you and me."

Charles took Marcus by the arm, and walked him back up the stairs. When their heads were above the level of the next floor, they could see Will standing at the other end of it, Evaporation Pen in hand.

"He doesn't have a range limit," Marcus said, as soon as they saw him.

"You definitely should have told me that sooner," Charles said. They fell to the ground, still on the stairs, as a red beam of light tore through the air above them, and caused pieces of ceiling to rain down everywhere.

"That's your one shot," Charles said, as he stood back up. "That's all you get." He slowly ascended the staircase, Marcus close behind him, and approached the man at the other end of the hall. He could see Will, still pressing the button of his Evaporation Pen, concern spreading through his face when it didn't work.

"You have to know the rules," Charles said. As he passed them, Charles spotted a few small, black objects placed at shoulder height halfway down the hall. "A nice little trap you set for me, Will. Let me tell you where you went wrong, two things: first of all, nothing you have will work right now, except your own two hands, and your own two 'feet'. Second of all, these are Identity Mines, am I right? Set to detonate on me? Do you have any idea how they work?"

Will did not respond, wouldn't play along. He just looked at Charles dead in the eyes, as the man approached. "It would have been extremely easy to program them to recognize a face. And that's probably how you think that they work. They probably would have worked, if that's what they did. But Karma was too confident. So confident, that its Identity Mines don't actually recognize faces. They recognize Karma Chips. And I don't have one of those."

Charles stopped ten feet away from Will. "If you wanted to beat me, you *would* have stood a much better chance as an engineer," he said. "Now Marcus, please finish this so we can go on." And he stepped aside to let Marcus pass.

"I can't believe you, Marcus," Will said, finally speaking. "I thought you were an officer."

"I am an officer," Marcus said. "I'm just not on your side."

"There's only one side that's right," Will said.

"I'm not a moral absolutist."

Will never lowered the Evaporation Pen that he was pointing at Charles and Marcus. Like he was mentally broken, he just kept pushing the button, even though nothing happened. When Marcus stood face to face with him, he could hear the man muttering over and over again, in a low voice, "Karma, I need you now."

"It's over, Will," Marcus said. "Stop saying that." And he hit him in the stomach, sending him through flying through the doorway he was standing in front of, into the hall it opened into.

"This isn't the way I would have it," Marcus said, as he hit him again on the ground, and again. Before he could hit him a fourth time, Will's Evaporation Pen went off, and Marcus was gone.

Charles could only watch—he couldn't believe what he was seeing. He took out his own Evaporation Pen, but when he saw that Will wasn't getting back up, he relaxed slightly. The Pen fell from Will's hand.

He walked up to the prostrate body and kicked the Evaporation Pen away from it. He grabbed Will's limp arm, and started pulling him down the hallway, back towards Karma.

"Normally I don't get upset, Will, but you've caught me under special circumstances. For the trouble you've given me, I'm going to make you watch Karma get destroyed." Will's head made loud banging noises as they went down the stairs. "Because I know how much you love Karma."

He propped Will up against a wall, on the opposite side of the room as the door to Karma, near the base of the stairs. "And to make it even better," Charles said, digging through Will's bag of weapons until he came out with a pair of high-torsion handcuffs. He verified the mark on the side that showed they weren't the normal variety. "Since these seem to work again. I'll demonstrate the barbarity of your arsenal to you." He cuffed one of Will's hands to the railing of the staircase, which extended out partially into the room. "Try not to move, or you'll regret it. Just watch."

He left Will there, and walked into the room with Karma, leaving his ghosts behind him. He was alone in a dark, entirely green room. "I'm here for you, Karma," Charles announced.

He didn't expect the voice that spoke back. "Welcome, Charles Darcy. I trust that you are healthy."

"That's beautiful. Marcus told me to expect you to sound like a person, but irony, from a machine? Not in my wildest dreams."

"Your dreams aren't that wild, at least none of the ones I've seen," Karma responded.

Hatred filled Charles' being. He took his Evaporation Pen back out from his pocket.

Karma continued, "Do you really think that what you're doing is right?"

"Let me hear your opinion on that one, just for the humor. How would you rate my actions, what value would you give them? You are the grand arbiter, after all."

"I'm afraid to say that they have no value."

Charles laughed harshly, for a long time. "No value. No value at all. That's why I'm going to kill you. Because no matter how much you learn, I think you'll judge the same way. And it will be the same thing on Mars, the same system. People will be allowed to procreate and pollute all they want, as long as they do Good Works every now and then, and you'll be buried so deep under the ground that no one would ever be able to try to change your mind, ever again. Whether I'm right or not, I came at the right time. It was now, or not at all."

"What will take my place, Charles Darcy? When I am gone? Do you have a plan? Everything I have done has been a necessity. People need to be economically limited somehow. People insist that they have basic freedoms. My system is a natural development of those two propositions, nothing more, nothing less. Nothing you will propose could do it better. I've made all of these considerations."

"It's good to see you lie, Karma. You don't believe in their basic freedoms either, these countless people. I saw you take away their Privacy Rooms, to save yourself. Did you really change the rule, back then, to let Will use his Evaporation Pen again, after he used it in a Room? Because it really surprised me. And furthermore, I'm impressed. You're expressing a high level of self-preservation."

"I do what needs to be done," Karma said.

"In that respect, as leaders, we're really not that different," Charles said. "It's just that I'd rather it was me. This Evaporation Pen, this death I give you, it's a tribute to what you've done." And he pulled the trigger of his Evaporation Pen, sweeping it across the room.

He never let go of the trigger, as hot as it became from the energy it was releasing, even when it began to burn his hand.

The green light died in a shower of sparks, and dust, and the back wall opened up to expose the afternoon sky, a mile above the earth. He held the trigger until the Pen stopped working, and he stood alone in the silence, with natural sunlight entering the room for the first time since it was built, although the Solar Kite blocked most of it from them.

He looked down at his hand, which had a severe, rectangular burn mark where he had been holding the Pen. "Carried away," he said quietly, to himself. He opened the door to leave the room.

18

ON THE OTHER side of the door, his remaining ghosts had just been Evaporated. For the split second that he had the door open, he could see a lonely arm, hanging by a chain from the handrail across the room. He saw Will Spector, damaged beyond repair yet still standing, holding the Evaporation Pen that must have been the one Charles left by where Marcus had died. It was an oversight he had made, in his anger. He closed the door again, staying in the room with the former Karma.

He quickly glanced at a watch on his wrist, to see how much time he had left. In two minutes, his Order would attempt to blow up the building, if they were still alive on the ground floor. Charles was supposed to be on his way back up to a Helicar, where a pilot was waiting for him. But if he couldn't get back out to the staircase, then he wouldn't be going to the roof.

He had two options. He could go back out in to the room, and attempt to shoot Will before Will shot him. And then he would have to quickly find his way back up to the roof, and hope that he made it in time. His other option was a Grappling Chain that he had in his left pocket, and the sunlit aperture in front of him, where Karma had been. He would be out of the building in seconds. He imagined that the likelihood of success was about the same for either option. And if he waited any longer, Will would come to him instead.

"Come out and die, Charles," Will shouted through the door.

"I think I'll just stay in here instead," Charles responded.

Will shot the door with his Evaporation Pen, and the barrier separating them turned to nothing. Charles pulled the Grappling Chain out of his pocket, and jumped out of the building. Two seconds later, he wished that he had practiced more with the thing, but he figured it out in time to shoot a link between him and a passing window, as he fell. When the Chain went taut, the window shattered and he had to retract and shoot it again, but it did slow his fall. He grazed the side of the building, shot again, and broke another window. The building was entirely windows.

It was only a matter of luck that Will had his Grappling Chain in his pocket, left there from when he decided it was helpful overcoming the short range of his stun gun. With one arm, he exchanged his Pen for the Chain, and jumped out the window after Charles.

Charles couldn't look up well enough to see that Will was following him, but he did hear smashing glass above him, and knew that he was coming after him. The kid was crazy. Charles collided with the building much harder than he had intended, about halfway down, and he was only barely conscious as he shot again, swinging laterally across the building. He had to land somewhere else.

Will's shoes had been shredded to nothing, exposing his robotic feet. He tried to use them to soften the impact of every time he ran into the side of the building, but with only one arm he was poorly coordinated, and hit his head a few times.

The wind became an ecstatic rush for a few seconds, and

then the twang of the Chain going taut, then the shattering of glass, the impact, the building, then all over again. At no point did Will think he was going to survive—he just wouldn't let Charles get away, no matter what happened to himself in the process. If he had a spare arm, he would have been shooting with his Evaporation Pen at the same time, but fate took his arm away. Distantly below him, he could see Charles making his way across the building, instead of falling straight down. Will couldn't do the same thing, he was barely holding on as it was.

The ground came quickly, for Will. He shot his Grappling Chain, one last time, and when he hit the wall of the building, he tried to jump up, as hard as he could. His mechanical legs went through the glass, destroying his right foot, and he couldn't have been more grateful for the complete absence of pain. When his feet reached the frame of the window, he found just enough leverage to jump, sending him flying away from the building.

He landed on a person that was standing on the sidewalk outside of the building, but he made it. He stood up as quickly as he could, and chased after Charles, limping on his broken foot.

Aaron was standing in amazement at the foot of Karma Tower, watching as two people fell down the side of the building, in a rain of glass. People around him were stopping to look up as well.

A woman next to him was saying to her husband, "My Karma Card isn't working."

Her husband didn't want to be distracted from watching, so

he answered irritably, "Have you been charging it?"

"The battery didn't die," she persisted. "It isn't working."

Another man, who had been listening to their conversation, added, "Hey, mine's not working either."

Aaron looked down at his own Card, only long enough to see that it wasn't working either, before looking back up to watch. He smiled. Maybe he would be free from the tyranny of Karma after all, before it was too late for him.

More and more people stopped to watch, and quickly the crowd was huge. Aaron and the people around him realized, all of them too late, that one of the two people would land right where they were standing. They didn't have time to react. A man landed directly on top of the woman that had spoken, sending her crashing to the ground. Her husband stared in dismay. The man that had been falling stood directly back up, and pushed his way out of the crowd, running to the other side of the building.

"My God," her husband was saying over and over again, still stunned.

Aaron got to his knees, by the broken woman. She was bleeding profusely from her head and arm, but still breathing. Aaron took his shirt off, tore it into pieces, and tried binding it around the wounds, to apply pressure. While he was doing it, he shouted, "Someone, call an ambulance. She's still alive."

"Can't," a man said. "The Cards don't work."

"Well, help me anyway. She's still alive. Where's the nearest subway? And the nearest hospital? If we take her ourselves, we can make it."

"Just stop," the husband said.

"What, what do you mean stop? She's still breathing," Aaron said. He looked up, from where he was kneeling, into the blank expression of the husband, looking down.

"If we just wait, the Cards might turn back on."

"If your Cards magically turned back on right now, and you immediately got an ambulance to come out here, chances are it would take just as long as if we took her ourselves. Except my way doesn't rely entirely on stupid chance." He had just finished fastening his compress around her head, and was getting frustrated with the people around him.

"I mean," her husband continued, "I'm sure it would be worth a lot of money, if Karma saw us saving her. So if we just wait…"

"She's your wife!" Aaron yelled, infuriated.

"We have bills," he stammered. "She would understand."

"I hate you, I hate all of you," Aaron said, as he lifted the woman up alone. "I pray to God, I really do, that karma really exists. Not that piece of shit computer you all believe in, but the real thing. You're all beautiful, well-adapted citizens now, but what then? I can only pray."

"Even if you go to the hospital," another man said, "if the Cards aren't working, it's pretty likely that people won't be able to help you there either."

"Won't be able? Won't be able? You're all able, you're just idiots. Against all odds, I might find another decent human being there. We'll just see. But that's not going to stop me now." He pushed his way through the crowd, carrying a limp, dying life in his hands.

"Can one of you assholes at least tell me where the nearest subway is?"

Charles ran as fast as he could, through the streets of New York City. He was trying to make it to the City Park, the place that he knew best, in hopes of having an advantage there. He could hear Will running close behind him, although he didn't dare turn around.

A red beam filled the space to the left of Charles' head. He was going to die. If he survived, it was because Will was shooting left-handed.

A huge explosion erupted behind them. Charles turned his head only long enough to see what it was, but he kept running as he did. He could see Karma Tower, not too far in the distance, begin to topple over. His Order had managed to blow it up. From the corner of his eye, he could see Will stop to turn around and watch.

Charles couldn't believe it. The young officer was entranced by the falling of the Tower. He thought about continuing to run, but if he did he left a witness to his crimes behind, and it was possible he would never have a chance to kill him again. It was also possible that Will would hear him running, and recover from his reverie. He felt insane as he did it, but he turned around and walked silently towards the man.

He didn't have any weapons of his own. His Grappling Chain could never kill a person, and he had used all the energy of his Evaporation Pen to destroy Karma. He didn't know what he would do. The closer to Will he got, the more nervous he became, but still the man didn't turn around. Charles was directly behind him.

From behind, Charles grabbed Will by his remaining wrist and pulled the Evaporation Pen towards them. It was a subtle movement that he almost missed, but with one finger he turned the range of the Pen all the way down, as he pulled with the others. At the same time, he whispered, "Shouldn't look back." And he pushed the button.

Nothing remained but a pair of metal legs. Charles couldn't help but breathe him in, since he was standing so close. He fainted.

A week later, Charles Darcy was standing on a podium, a microphone in front of him, addressing the entire world. Cameras surrounded him, broadcasting to televisions everywhere.

He said, "I know that I said I wanted to disappear from the public eye, the last time that I was on television. I said that I wanted to just be an ordinary citizen, doing what was in my power to serve the common good. But that was before the destruction of Karma, just one week ago. This last week has been a very hard week for everyone. Chaos everywhere. If nothing is done, and very soon, our entire society could unravel. I saw a great public need, so I came back.

"We need to decide how to move forward from this, as a people. We don't have Karma to help us anymore. And there are a lot of things to decide. How do we re-establish a world economy, when it has fallen apart? What do we do with Mars, which, as we speak, is in a critical state of development? It's not as simple as building another Karma. That could take years. And, from what the events of a week ago demonstrate, perhaps another Karma isn't entirely safe anyway. The terrorist organization that destroyed it is still at large, since no measures are in place to combat them.

"In times of great emergency, what the Romans would do—and this is a very long time ago—was to elect one private citizen, called the Magister Populi. Like Cincinnatus. That one person would see the Roman Republic through its hardships, when a group of people, split by disagreements, would have failed. When the emergency was gone, the Magister Populi would give the power back to the people and become an ordinary citizen once more. And the Roman Empire became one of the strongest nations in history, they made it through those hardships.

"It's far from modest, and I apologize for that, but what I ask is that you let me be your Magister Populi. Give me authority, I will see us through this hardship, and when we are through it I will give it back. I'm only saying this because I don't see many other options. Many of the heroes that we knew have died, but I'm still here. And I won't let you down.

"I'll leave the choice to all of you. If I've convinced any of you, both in the past and right now, that I am the person that these times call for, then tell me. Consider your options. And I'll be waiting."

He stepped down from the podium, bowed modestly, and left the stage.

Made in the USA
Middletown, DE
12 July 2022

68996801R00113